Eric S. Robertson

The Children of the Poets

An anthology from English and American writers of three centuries

Eric S. Robertson

The Children of the Poets
An anthology from English and American writers of three centuries

ISBN/EAN: 9783337386023

Printed in Europe, USA, Canada, Australia, Japan

Cover: Foto ©Andreas Hilbeck / pixelio.de

More available books at **www.hansebooks.com**

The
Children of the Poets

AN ANTHOLOGY

FROM

ENGLISH AND AMERICAN WRITERS OF
THREE CENTURIES.

Edited, with Introduction

BY

ERIC S. ROBERTSON.

LONDON:
Walter Scott, 24 Warwick Lane, Paternoster Row,
AND NEWCASTLE-ON-TYNE.
1886.

CONTENTS.

CONTENTS.

CONTENTS.

CONTENTS.

CONTENTS. xi

CONTENTS.

CONTENTS. xiii

WITH AFFECTION

I INSCRIBE THIS LITTLE VOLUME TO

𝕵. 𝕻. 𝕯.,

MY OLDEST FRIEND,

IN REMEMBRANCE OF OUR BOYHOOD.

E. S. R.

Introduction.

ALES from Arabia describe the wise magician whose cunning ear, held close to the ground in the hot heart of an African desert, could detect the pattering of children's feet on the pavement of Bagdad, discriminating voice from voice in the shouts that accompanied their games. It is harder for us to find, throughout ancient literature, many echoes of youthful laughter or glimpses of youthful smiles. The instinct that links parent to child must always have been one of the best marked sentiments in primitive, as it is in modern writings; but the child by itself, as a study for the artist, either in words or in plastic and graphic reproductive processes, is an invention of the moderns. It seems

to be the case that as the world grows older it more and more takes interest in things that are young. The earliest poetry never received so much attention as it does now. Prehistoric art has in our days a multitude of students. We of this critical age are searching into the beginnings of things ; and one of our discoveries is, that the most entrancing method of studying humanity's beginnings lies in the freshest problems God sends us. The whole secret of humanity can be examined in an infant, whether by laborious inductions of science like Darwin's or by subtle divinations like Victor Hugo's. In the early world, the general spirit of man was more childlike, and tender lives were looked at with less wistful eyes than our own. But we, with our enlarged record of great nations and great religions come to dust, and the dark of futurity still before us—we, less filled with the joy of living, turn with increasing interest to the capacities for love and faith, the sense of the goodness of existence, and the longing expectancy of a growing brightness, that make up the spirit of childhood.

It is true that if we do put our ears very close to the ground, and listen intently, we can catch a few notes of child-humanity from far lands and times; and these show us, as we might expect, that in every age and clime the young resemble each other closely in their feelings and habits. In Homer we find boys building sand castles by the sea, or hunting for wasps' nests, as our own children might do. The old poet describes the crowd of gay young rustics who attempt with their cudgels to drive the wandering donkey out of a corn-field ; and sulky Ajax facing the Trojans is likened to that donkey. Hector at the Scæan Gate enacts with wife and child the most beautiful tableau of parental affection that ancient literature affords : and even the selfish nature of Achilles has noted the sorrows of a little maid :—

> " Why weeps Patroclus like an infant girl,
>   That prays her mother, by whose side she runs,
>   To take her up, and, clinging to her gown,
>   Impedes her way, and still with tearful eyes
>   Looks in her face, until she takes her up ? "

It is this Achilles who in early days climbs on the knees of his father's guest, clamours for a sip from his goblet, and spills the wine over his bib. The boy Ulysses walks with his father through the home-garden, learning the names of trees and flowers, and glancing proudly at the plot of ground he has had given him—all to himself. Sweetest of Homer's young folks, Nausicaa is herself hardly

b

more than a child when the travelled hero rises from his bed of leaves to disturb her game of ball. Few, few are the references to childhood in ancient literature so natural as Homer's. One indeed is so very human that the fragment containing it will never be forgotten—

> " Hesperus brings all things back
> Which the daylight made us lack—
> Brings the sheep and goats to rest,
> Brings the baby to the breast."

These lines of Sappho's remind us that perhaps the first attempt at song that sprang from human lips was a lullaby, and the first notion of metre derived itself from the rocking of an infant in its mother's arms or in a cradle.

Such hints show us that the Greeks took the sweetness of childhood as a patent fact, and cared to analyse it no more than they would have wished to grasp at a cloud in the blue. In art they held equally aloof from direct study of child-being. But the Infant Bacchus sporting among submissive beasts of the forest makes a picture that takes from one of the least lovely of old superstitions much of its grossness, and Cupid by the side of Venus enables us to forget that most of her sighs are wanton.

Far different, however, is the relation of mother to child in the first great transition of art from classicism. The Goose Boy of the Vatican collection, and here and there a stray example of a like kind, may suggest that Greeks and Romans never quite forgot to dally with children's beauty in art ; but in the middle ages the child was suppressed, save in the Church. In sculpture the Church gave us little more than grotesques from the hands of cathedral masons, and the wooden *bambini*, the worship of which was eagerly taken up by the common people, as it still is—let any one witness who steps into the Aracoeli Church, at Rome in the Christmas time. In painting, the Church allowed only emaciated Christs designed in stiff lines full of symbolism. And the Virgin, whose effigy was long prohibited in every form, was scarcely attempted save in a symbolic style till Cimabue's time. When all Florence turned out to see Cimabue's Virgin and Child for an altar at Santa Maria Novella, the excitement was due to the fact that art was beginning to revolt from theological abstractions in favour of ordinary flesh and blood. Giotto next tried to paint the Infant Saviour naturally. Giotto draws Him laughing or crying, and even playing with the symbolic apple held in his hand. In sculpture, somewhat later, the

Renaissance of classical forms inspired Donatello with his singing children for the Florentine Duomo, Luca della Robbia with his child-fantasies in *terra cotta*, and John of Bologna with his bronze Cupids.

But Raphael's transcendent genius explored the mysterious beauty of this theme. Never did the monachism upheld by the Church receive a deadlier blow, save from Luther, than in the studies of Madonna and Child painted by Raphael. Abstractions vanished from his canvases, though he retained many of the symbols. His Madonna was a flesh-and-blood woman of the people, with a healthily-developed child held to her ample bosom. Well might the Church have been chary of allowing artists to abandon the theologically abstract method of representing a mysterious miracle-working Virgin with her still more mysterious Child. In Raphael's pictures the most mysterious thing about the Madonna is her exquisite womanly beauty, and the worshippers who looked upon the babes he depicted for them felt that he was drawing portraits from their own homes. The blessings of a man's home—wife and child—were what Raphael's best canvases preached in every great church of Italy.

While art was thus developing the cult of childhood, literature had scarcely awakened to the subject. It is true that church dogmas were then enshrining themselves in legends of varying beauty, and the Holy Child perched on the broad shoulders of St. Christopher, or descending to the outstretched arms of the ecstatic St. Francis of Assisi, becomes an object of interest to the poet, apart from the religious doctrines with which such appearances are connected. In Troubadour poetry, of course, we have the page, but he is so artificial a specimen of youth (even in his youngest stage) that he is not worth staying to consider. Of interest in common childhood around them the penmen of the dark ages were almost wholly devoid ; and probably it would be hard to produce from a century before the fifteenth any passage of mark on the subject save Dante's (in the "Inferno"), copied by Chaucer—

> " Of erl Hugilin of Pise the languour
> Ther may no tonge telle for pité.
> But litel out of Pise stant a tour,
> In whiche tour in prisoun put was he ;
> And with him been his litel children thre,
> Theldest skarsely fyf yer was of age ;
> Allas ! fortune ! it was gret cruelté
> Suche briddes to put in such a cage."

The story of Ugolino's starvation with his babes

is told by our poet—through the Monke's lips—in brief, but,

> " Who-so will hiere it in a lenger wise,
>   Rede the gret poet of Itaile,
>   That high Dauuté, for he can it devise
>   Fro poynt to poynt nought oon word wil he fayle."

Chaucer likewise gives us glimpses of his sunny sympathies in the Prioresse's Tale of a martyred Christian boy—

> " Ther was in Acy, in a gret citee
>   Amonges Cristen folk a Jewerye,
>   Susteyned by a lord of that contré,
>   For foul usure and lucre of felonye,
>   Hateful to Crist, and to his compaignye ;
>   And thurgh the strete men mighte ride and wende,
>   For it was fre, and open at everiche end.
>   A litel scole of Cristen folk ther stood
>   Doun at the forther end, in which ther were
>   Children an heep y-comen of Cristen blood,
>   That lered in that scole, yer by yere,
>   Such maner doctrine as men usede there ;
>   This is to saye, to synge and to rede,
>   As smale childer doon in her childhede.
>   Among these children was a widow sone,
>   A litel clergeoun, that seve yer was of age,
>   That day by day to scole was his wone ;

> And eek also, wherso he saugh thymage
> Of Cristes moder, had he in usage,
> As him was taught, to knele adoun, and saye
> His *Ave Maria*, as he gotn by the waye."

The little scholar's hymn-singing is resented by the Jews of the quarter, and old Satan

> "That hath in Jewes hert his waspis nest,"

brings about his murder. On the whole, the story is repulsive—

> " Ther he with throte i-corve lay upright,
> He *Alma redemptoris* gan to synge
> So lowde, that al the place bigan to rynge."

Among our early English writers, we might have expected Spenser to have given evidence of sympathy for child life ; but he has not even left us an elegy upon the child he lost in the terrible Irish fire. Sir Walter Raleigh hands down to us grotesque lines to his son about the gallows, and Gower begins a respectable poem "On the Nativity of Christ," thus—

> " Rorate, Coeli desuper !
> Heavens, distil your balmy show'rs,
> For now is risen the bricht day-star
> For the Rose-May, flow'r of flow'rs :

The clear sun, whom no cloud devours,
Surmounting Phoebus in the east,
Is coming of his heavenly tow'rs ;
Et nobis Puer natus est."

The first really fine child-poem in our literature is Southwell's " Burning Babe." Its exquisitely pure feeling, and the mystic light and heat of the language, render the poem so impressive that it can be learnt off by heart after two or three readings. Occurring so early in the present collection, the " Burning Babe" really shows us the point from which both the literature and the art of modern times had to start, in their treatment of the child—the glorification of young Jesus. Readers of this volume will note that I have chosen to represent Mr. William Sharp among poets of our own day, with fine lines that have a note somewhat like that of South-well's piece, though their composition was unin-fluenced by it. Southwell's noble spirit endured the wounds and thorns, like his Master : love was the fire, sighs were the smoke, the ashes—" shame and scorn." After years of torture in a dungeon, all which he endured steadfastly as a martyr for Catholicism, he was condemned to death in 1594, and the hands of bigots hanged him in company with a highwayman, afterwards disembowelling and quartering his body. Sir Edward Coke conducted

the shameful prosecution of this high-souled Jesuit,
with whose family, by the way, Percy Bysshe
Shelley was connected by descent. While Southwell
was rotting in his dungeon, in the reign of good
Queen Bess, Shakespeare was playing his many
parts ; and about the time of the Romanist martyr's
execution, the dramatist's "King John" was being
finished. It is in this play that Shakespeare
gives us his only notable child-character, and the
scene in which Arthur's "artless eloquence" pleads
with Hubert against the decree of his malignant
uncle remains one of the most deeply-moving
passages in our dramatic literature. Strong as it
is, however, it is not nature. Is this the language
of a child, however noble of blood and valiant in
bearing ?—

" *Arthur.* The instrument is cold,
And would not harm me.
    Hubert. I can heat it, boy.
    Arthur. No, in good sooth ; the fire is dead with grief,
Being create for comfort, to be us'd
In undeserv'd extremes : See else yourself ;
There is no malice in this burning coal ;
The breath of heaven hath blown his spirit out
And strew'd repentant ashes on his head.
    Hubert. But with my breath I can revive it, boy.
    Arthur. And if you do, you will but make it blush,
And glow with shame of your proceedings, Hubert :

> Nay it, perchance, will sparkle in your eyes ;
> And, like a dog that is compell'd to fight,
> Snatch at his master that doth tarre him on.
> All things, that you should use to do me wrong,
> Deny their office : only you do lack
> That mercy which fierce fire, and iron, extends,
> Creatures of note for mercy-lacking uses."

A most Euphuistic young hero, this, to indulge in so many brave sallies of fancy at such a moment of agony ! This is not the stuff of which children are made ; nor has the well-nigh all-creative genius of Shakespeare given us any deep readings of child-nature. Stray allusions to children occur throughout his plays with more or less effect : in " King John " we have that pathetic moan of a mother, when Constance speaks :—

> " Grief fills the room up of my absent child ;
> Lies in his bed ; walks up and down with me ;
> Puts on his pretty looks, repeats his words,
> Remembers me in all his gracious parts,
> Stuffs out his vacant garments with his form ;
> Then have I reason to be fond of grief."

And poet's strength describes the murdered Princes of the Tower thus, albeit the speakers are supposed to be rude-witted varlets :—

" ' O thus,' quoth Dighton, ' lay the gentle babes '—
' Thus, thus,' quoth Forrest, ' folding one another '
Within their alabaster innocent arms :
Their lips were four red roses on a stalk,
Which, in their summer beauty, kiss'd each other.
A book of prayer on their pillow lay ;
Which once,' quoth Forrest, ' almost chang'd my mind ;
But, O ! the devil '—there the villain stopp'd ·
When Dighton thus told on, ' We smothered
The most replenished sweet work of nature
That, from the prime creation, e'er she fram'd.' "

The pity of this tale is only approached by the old
ballads of "The Children in the Wood" (some
say, the disguised history of Richard the Third's
little nephews), and "The Cruel Mother," otherwise called, "Fine Flowers of the Valley." I
have been unwilling to give this last ballad in the
body of the book, because of its repellent subject—
the murder a mother commits on her new-born
babe. The concluding verses of the powerful story
may be quoted :—

" She's howket a grave by the light o' the moon,
    Fine flowers in the valley ;
And there she's buried her sweet babe in,
    And the green leaves they grow rarely.

As she was going to the church,
    Fine flowers in the valley ;

She saw a sweet babe in the porch,
And the green leaves they grow rarely.

' O sweet babe, if thou wert mine,'
Fine flowers in the valley,
' I wad cleed thee in silk and sabelline ; '
And the green leaves they grow rarely.

' O mother mine, when I was thine,'
Fine flowers in the valley,
' You did na prove to me sae kind,'
And the green leaves they grow rarely.

' But now I'm in the heavens hie,'
Fine flowers in the valley,
' And ye have the pains o' hell to dree '—
And the green leaves they grow rarely."

Of the writers who followed the Elizabethans, Quarles will be missed from this collection. He wrote but one child-poem of power, and its merits are so overgrown by conceits that I have omitted it. It is entitled "On the Infancy of our Saviour," and in some respects resembles the quaint poem on the same subject that I have drawn from the works of Crashaw. Quarles's verses commence in this fashion :—

" Hail, blessed Virgin, full of heavenly grace,
Blest above all that sprang from human race ;
Whose heaven-saluted womb brought forth in One,
A blessed Saviour and a blessed Son.

O what ravishment 't had been to see
Thy little Saviour perking on thy knee !
To see him nuzzle in thy Virgin Breast !
His milk-white body all unclad, undressed ;
To see thy busy fingers clothe and wrap
His spradling limbs in thy indulgent lap !
To see his desperate Eyes, with Childish grace,
Smiling upon his smiling mother's face ;
And, when his forward strength began to bloom,
To see him diddle up and down the room ! "

George Herbert also lacks a place in this volume ;
he wrote no child-poem. But one who acknowledged him as master, Henry Vaughan the Silurist,
must rank here among the greatest of childhood's
poets. He it was who, feeling

"Through all this fleshly dress
Bright shoots of everlastingness,"

sang first of the life anterior to childhood that forms
dim "shadows of eternity," in Wordsworth's "Ode
on Immortality." That many of Vaughan's ideas
are reproduced in Wordsworth's poem, critics
have long acknowledged : that the reproduction
was consciously evolved by the later poet, no one
could affirm : but the fact has been asserted by
Trench that of Henry Vaughan's "Silex Scintillans"
(the book containing "The Retreat") Wordsworth possessed a well-thumbed copy ; and this

copy was down in the sale catalogue of his library. There seems no reason to doubt, therefore, that Vaughan's "Retreat" not only is in itself a treasure to our literature, but directly inspired the still nobler lay of him who first in the world appreciated the full value of childhood's theme— William Wordsworth. It may be noted that in his "Corruption," a poem also included in "Silex Scintillans," Vaughan reiterates the idea of soul-transmigration.

> "Sure it was so.   Man in those early days
> Was not all stone and earth ;
> He shined a little, and by those weak rays
> Had some glimpses of his birth.
> He saw Heaven o'er his head and knew from whence
> He came—condemnèd—hither,
> And, as first love draws strongest, so from hence
> His mind sure progressed thither."

Star-like childhood had many attractions to the visionary Silurist, and in his "Lament" for a younger brother we have touches of nature that are as perfect, and as modern in feeling, as anything of Wordsworth's or Tennyson's—

> "There's not a wind can stir,
>   Or beam pass by,
>   But straight I think—though far—
>   Thy hand is nigh."

It may serve some students if I draw attention to
the fine continuation of Vaughan's and Wordsworth's thought upon the dawn of being that is
contained in Joaquin Miller's " Unknown Tongue."

It would surely be needless for me to dwell on
the variety of beauty with which Wordsworth has
adorned the study of children. Jean Paul says, " I
love God and every little child." Wordsworth was
not, in the general, a man from whom human sympathies welled profusely, but it might be said of
him that he truly loved nature and childhood.
Childhood was the great theme of his erring
follower and child-like brother-poet, Hartley Coleridge ; so had it been the recurrent theme of Blake's
tenderly fantastic genius ; and since their time this
whole subject has grown, till a book of verse is now
hardly complete without its tribute to the very
young. Into the varied merits of the recent poems
here collected I will excuse myself from entering,
for many reasons, some of them obvious. I will
only say that I have striven to represent American
writers in my later pages as freely as possible, and
believe that Mrs. Piatt's poems, in particular, will
come to many readers, fresh, as well as delightful
contributions from across the ocean. Occasionally
I have introduced pieces rather because of their
happy choice of subject than for their strength of

poetic treatment, believing that mothers, who are all poets in their children, will feel them to be fuller of beauty than some more carefully finished poems signed with names honoured everywhere. These less known excerpts are nearly all the work of women, and hence perhaps their peculiar tenderness; for of male poets in general George Eliot might perhaps have said with some truth what she said of bachelors : " A bachelor's children are always young ; they're immortal children, always lisping, wandering, helpless, and with a chance of turning out good."

I have eschewed translations and extracts from dramatic works. In three cases poems have been quoted in an abridged form. Following the late Menella Smedley's poems is a fine contribution from a writer who, adopting the signature of " A," collaborated with Miss Smedley in producing " Poems written for a Child," and " The Child World." These books enjoy large circulations, and " A.'s " identity is a pretty open secret. Nevertheless " A.'s " wish is to remain anonymous in this volume. I have vainly endeavoured to ascertain the name or whereabouts of the anonymous writer who brought out " A Child's Life " some years ago : but I have ventured, without authority, to cull two pieces from this delightful volume, and trust that if their author happens to look through this collection, the appropriation will be condoned. In all other cases I believe I have secured from living authors the right to publish the pieces I have chosen from their works. The obligation I thus lie under to many distinguished writers is a great one; and I must express a warm sense of gratitude for the favours extended to me by almost every author, from Lord Tennyson to the youngest. From "Whistle-Binkie," that book of Scottish songs which first put into print William Miller's immortal "Willie Winkie," I should have been glad to make a wider selection of subjects; but it appeared to me that I should best please the majority of my readers by minimising the number of dialect poems in the book.

I think I may claim to have made a fair search through our literature in forming this collection. Its compilation has consumed so many of my more leisurely hours during the last few years, that only a love of the labour has repaid me. In gathering many poems of infancy together, we lose something of the soft brightness in each; it is like accumulating dew-drops. However, beauty remains: and a volume in which are to be found studies of dawning lives by most of the great English poets is likely

c

to receive kindly welcome from such readers as have discovered in the deep friendship of some wise child the most delicate of spiritual boons.

It remains for me to add my recognition of the fact that much of the poetry of childhood has been written in prose that does not come within my editorial scope. That poetry is not distinct from prose is a doctrine as old as Coleridge; but let the reader who wishes to see how much poetry can be contained in a little prose find and treasure that fragment of biography by the late Dr. John Brown, called " Marjorie Fleming," a pamphlet of twenty pages, and the best book about a child that ever was written.

ERIC S. ROBERTSON.

3 ST. JAMES'S STREET, S. W.

THE

CHILDREN OF THE POETS.

We meet wi' blythesome and kythesome cheerie weans,
Daffin' and laughin' far adoon the leafy lanes,
Wi' gowans and buttercups buskin' the thorny wands—
Sweetly singin' wi' the flower-branch wavin' in their
*   hands.*

—WILLIAM MILLER.

The Children of the Poets.

———◆———

THE AGE OF CHILDREN HAPPIEST.

Laid in my quiet bed in study as I were,
I saw within my troubled head a heap of thoughts appear,
And every thought did show so lively in mine eyes,
That now I sighed, and then I smiled, as cause of thoughts
    did rise.
I saw the little boy in thought, how oft that he
Did wish of God, to 'scape the rod, a tall young man to be;
The young man eke that feels his bones with pain opprest,
How he would be a rich old man, to live and be at rest!
The rich old man that sees his end draw on so sore,
How would he be a boy again to live so much the more.
Whereat full oft I smiled, to see how all those three,
From boy to man, from man to boy, would chop and
    change degree.

Earl of Surrey.

21

CHILD-SONG.

Sleepe, babie mine, Desire's nurse, Beautie, singeth;
Thy cries, O babie, set mine head on aking.
The babe cries, "Way, thy love doth keepe me waking."
Lully, lully, my babe, Hope cradle bringeth
Unto my children alway, good rest taking.
The babe cries, "Way, thy love doth keepe me waking."
Since, babie mine, from me thy watching springeth,
Sleepe then, a little, pap Content is making.
The babe cries, "Nay, for that abide I waking."

Sir Philip Sidney.

A SWEET LULLABY.

Come, little babe! come, silly soul!
   Thy father's shame, thy mother's grief:
Born, as I doubt, to all our dole,
   And to thyself unhappy chief;
Sing lullaby, and lap it warm,
Poor soul that thinks no creature harm!

Thou little think'st and less dost know
   The cause of all thy mother's moan;
Thou want'st the wit to wail her woe,
   And I myself am all alone.
Why dost thou weep? Why dost thou wail?
And know'st not yet what thou dost ail.

Come, little wretch! ah, silly heart!
   Mine only joy! What can I more?
If there be any wrong thy smart,
   That may the destinies implore,—

'Twas I, I say, against my will;
I wail the time, but be thou still!

And dost thou smile?   O thy sweet face!
    Would God himself he might thee see:
No doubt thou would'st soon purchase grace,
    I know right well, for thee and me.
But come to Mother, Babe! and play:
For father false is fled away.

Nicholas Breton.

THE BURNING BABE.

As I in hoary winter's night stood shivering in the snow,
Surprised I was with sudden heat, which made my heart
    to glow;
And lifting up a fearful eye to view what fire was near,
A pretty babe, all burning bright, did in the air appear;
Who, scorchèd with excessive heat, such floods of tears
    did shed,
As though his floods should quench his flames which with
    his tears were fed:—
"Alas!" quoth He, "but newly born, in fiery heats I fry,
Yet none approach to warm their hearts or feel my fire
    but I!
My faultless breast the furnace is, the fuel, wounding
    thorns;
Love is the fire, and sighs the smoke, the ashes, shame
    and scorns;
The fuel Justice layeth on, and Mercy blows the coals,
The metal in this furnace wrought are men's defilèd souls,

For which, as now on fire I am, to work them to their
    good,
So will I melt into a bath to wash them in my blood !"—
With this He vanished out of sight, and swiftly shrunk
    away ;
And straight I callèd unto mind that it was Christmas-day.

Robert Southwell.

SEPHESTIA'S SONG TO HER CHILD.

(*From "Menaphon."*)

WEEP not, my wanton, smile upon my knee ;
When thou art old, there's grief enough for thee.
    Mother's wag, pretty boy,
    Father's sorrow, father's joy ;
    When thy father first did see
    Such a boy by him and me,
    He was glad, I was woe ;
    Fortune changèd made him so,
    When he left his pretty boy,
    Last his sorrow, first his joy.

Weep not, my wanton, smile upon my knee ;
When thou art old, there's grief enough for thee.
    Streaming tears that never stint,
    Like pearl-drops from a flint,
    Fell by course from his eyes,
    That one another's place supplies ;
    Thus he grieved in every part,
    Tears of blood fell from his heart
    When he left his pretty boy,
    Father's sorrow, father's joy.

Weep not, my wanton, smile upon my knee ;
When thou art old, there's grief enough for thee.
    The wanton smiled, father wept,
    Mother cried, baby leapt ;
    More he crowed, more we cried,
    Nature could not sorrow hide :
    He must go, he must kiss
    Child and mother, baby bliss,
    For he left his pretty boy,
    Father's sorrow, father's joy.
Weep not, my wanton, smile upon my knee ;
When thou art old, there's grief enough for thee.

Robert Greene.

ON MY FIRST DAUGHTER.

HERE lies, to each her parents' ruth,
Mary, the daughter of their youth ;
Yet all heaven's gifts being heaven's due,
It makes the father less to rue.
At six months' end she parted hence,
With safety of her innocence ;
Whose soul Heaven's queen (whose name she bears),
In comfort of her mother's tears,
Hath placed among her virgin train :
Where, while that, severed, doth remain,
This grave partakes the fleshly birth ;
Which cover lightly, gentle earth !

Ben Jonson.

ON MY FIRST SON.

FAREWELL, thou child of my right hand, and joy :
   My sin was too much hope of thee, loved boy :
Seven years thou wert lent to me, and I thee pay,
   Exacted by thy faith on the just day.
O, could I lose all father now ! for why
   Will man lament the state he should envy ?
To have so soon 'scaped world's and flesh's rage,
   And if no other misery, yet age !
Rest in soft peace, and asked, say here doth lie
   Ben Jonson his best piece of poetry,
For whose sake henceforth all his vows be such
   As what he loves may never like too much.

Ben Jonson.

SLEEP, BABY, SLEEP !

SLEEP, baby, sleep ! what ails my dear ?
   What ails my darling thus to cry ?
Be still, my child, and lend thine ear
   To hear me sing thy lullaby.
My pretty lamb, forbear to weep ;
Be still, my dear ; sweet baby, sleep.

Thou blessed soul, what canst thou fear ?
   What thing to thee can mischief do ?
Thy God is now thy father dear,
   His holy Spouse thy mother too.
Sweet baby, then, forbear to weep ;
Be still, my babe ; sweet baby, sleep.

Though thy conception was in sin,
  A sacred bathing thou hast had ;
And though thy birth unclean hath been,
  A blameless babe thou now art made.
Sweet baby, then, forbear to weep ;
Be still, my dear ; sweet baby, sleep.

While thus thy lullaby I sing,
  For thee great blessings ripening be ;
Thine eldest brother is a King,
  And hath a kingdom bought for thee.
Sweet baby, then, forbear to weep ;
Be still, my babe ; sweet baby, sleep.

Sweet baby, sleep, and nothing fear ;
  For whosoever thee offends
By thy protector threatened are,
  And God and angels are thy friends.
Sweet baby, then, forbear to weep ;
Be still, my babe ; sweet baby, sleep.

When God with us was dwelling here,
  In little babes He took delight ;
Such innocents as thou, my dear,
  Are ever precious in His sight.
Sweet baby, then, forbear to weep ;
Be still, my babe ; sweet baby, sleep.

A little infant once was He ;
  And strength in weakness then was laid
Upon His virgin mother's knee,
  That power to thee might be convey'd.
Sweet baby, then, forbear to weep;
Be still, my babe; sweet baby, sleep.

.

In this thy frailty and thy need
   He friends and helpers doth prepare,
Which thee shall cherish, clothe, and feed,
   For of thy weal they tender are.
Sweet baby, then, forbear to weep;
Be still, my babe ; sweet baby, sleep.

The King of kings, when He was born,
   Had not so much for outward ease ;
By Him such dressings were not worn,
   Nor such-like swaddling clothes as these.
Sweet baby, then, forbear to weep;
Be still, my babe; sweet baby, sleep.

Within a manger lodged thy Lord,
   Where oxen lay, and asses fed ;
Warm rooms we do to thee afford,
   An easy cradle for a bed.
Sweet baby, then, forbear to weep;
Be still, my babe; sweet baby, sleep.

The wants that He did then sustain
   Have purchased wealth, my babe, for thee ;
And by His torments and His pain
   Thy rest and ease securèd be.
My baby, then, forbear to weep;
Be still, my babe; sweet baby, sleep.

Thou hast, yet more, to perfect this,
   A promise and an earnest got
Of gaining everlasting bliss,
   Though thou, my babe, perceiv'st it not.
Sweet baby, then, forbear to weep;
Be still, my babe ; sweet baby, sleep.

                     George Wither.

THE BABES IN THE WOOD.

Now ponder well, you parents dear,
These words which I shall write ;
A doleful story you shall hear
In time brought forth to light.
A gentleman of good account
In Norfolk dwelt of late,
Who did in honour far surmount
Most men of his estate.

Sore sick he was and like to die,
No help his life could save ;
His wife by him as sick did lie,
And both possest one grave.
No love between these two was lost,
Each was to other kind ;
In love they lived, in love they died,
And left two babes behind :

The one a fine and pretty boy
Not passing three years old,
The other a girl more young than he,
And framed in beauty's mould.
The father left his little son,
As plainly did appear,
When he to perfect age should come,
Three hundred pounds a-year.

And to his little daughter Jane
Five hundred pounds in gold,
To be paid down on marriage-day,
Which might not be controll'd.

But if the children chance to die
Ere they to age should come,
Their uncle should possess their wealth ;
For so the will did run.

" Now, brother," said the dying man,
" Look to my children dear,
Be good unto my boy and girl,
No friends else have they here :
To God and you I recommend
My children dear this day ;
But little while be sure we have
Within this world to stay.

" You must be father and mother both,
And uncle, all in one ;
God knows what will become of them
When I am dead and gone."
With that bespake their mother dear :
" O brother kind," quoth she,
" You are the man must bring our babes
To wealth or misery.

" And if you keep them carefully,
Then God will you reward ;
But if you otherwise should deal,
God will your deeds regard."
With lips as cold as any stone
They kiss'd their children small :
" God bless you both, my children dear ! "
With that the tears did fall.

These speeches then their brother spake
To this sick couple there :
" The keeping of your little ones,
Sweet sister, do not fear ;

God never prosper me nor mine,
Nor ought else that I have,
If I do wrong your children dear
When you are laid in grave ! "

The parents being dead and gone,
The children home he takes,
And brings them straight into his house,
Where much of them he makes.
He had not kept these pretty babes
A twelvemonth and a day,
But, for their wealth, he did devise
To make them both away.

He bargain'd with two ruffians strong,
Which were of furious mood,
That they should take these children young
And slay them in a wood.
He told his wife an artful tale :
He would the children send
To be brought up in London town
With one that was his friend.

Away then went those pretty babes
Rejoicing at that tide,
Rejoicing with a merry mind
They should on cock-horse ride.
They prate and prattle pleasantly,
As they ride on the way,
To those that should their butchers be,
And work their lives' decay :

So that the pretty speech they had
Made murder's heart relent ;
And they that undertook the deed
Full sore did now repent.

Yet one of them, more hard of heart,
Did vow to do his charge,
Because the wretch that hirèd him
Had paid him very large.

The other won't agree thereto,
So here they fall to strife ;
With one another they did fight
About the children's life :
And he that was of mildest mood
Did slay the other there,
Within an unfrequented wood ;
The babes did quake for fear !

He took the children by the hand,
Tears standing in their eye,
And bade them straightway follow him,
And look they did not cry ;
And two long miles he led them on,
While they for food complain :
" Stay here," quoth he ; " I'll bring you bread
When I come back again."

These pretty babes, with hand in hand,
Went wandering up and down ;
But never more could see the man
Approaching from the town.
Their pretty lips with blackberries
Were all besmear'd and dyed ;
And when they saw the darksome night,
They sat them down and cried.

Thus wander'd these poor innocents,
Till death did end their grief ;
In one another's arms they died,
As wanting due relief :

No burial this pretty pair
From any man receives,
Till Robin Redbreast piously
Did cover them with leaves.

And now the heavy wrath of God
Upon their uncle fell ;
Yea, fearful fiends did haunt his house—
His conscience felt an hell :
His barns were fired, his goods consumed,
His lands were barren made,
His cattle died within the field,
And nothing with him stay'd.

And in a voyage to Portugal
Two of his sons did die ;
And, to conclude, himself was brought
To want and misery :
He pawn'd and mortgaged all his land
Ere seven years came about,
And now at last this wicked act
Did by this means come out :

The fellow that did take in hand
These children for to kill,
Was for a robbery judged to die—
Such was God's blessed will :
Who did confess the very truth,
As here hath been display'd :
The uncle having died in jail,
Where he for debt was laid.

You that executors be made,
And overseers eke,
Of children that be fatherless,
And infants mild and meek,

Take you example by this thing,
And yield to each his right,
Lest God with such-like misery
Your wicked minds requite.

Old Ballad.

IN THE HOLY NATIVITY OF OUR LORD GOD.

Hymn Sung by the Shepherds.

THE HYMN.

Chorus.

COME, we shepherds, whose blest sight
Hath met Love's noon in Nature's night ;
Come, lift we up our loftier song
And wake the sun that lies too long.

To all our world of well-stol'n joy
He slept, and dreamt of no such thing,
　While we found out heaven's fairer eye,
And kissed the cradle of our King.
　Tell him he rises now too late
　To show us ought worth looking at.

　Tell him we now can show him more
Than he e'er showed to mortal sight ;
　Than he himself e'er saw before,
Which to be seen needs not his light.

　Tell him, Tityrus, where th' hast been,
　Tell him, Thyrsis, what th' hast seen.

TITYRUS.

Gloomy night embraced the place
Where the noble Infant lay;
   The Babe looked up and showed His face:
In spite of darkness it was day.
   It was Thy day, Sweet! and did rise
Not from the East, but from Thine eyes.
        Chorus.—It was Thy day, Sweet, etc.

THYRSIS.

Winter chid aloud, and sent
The angry North to wage his wars;
   The North forgot his fierce intent,
And left perfumes instead of scars.
   By those sweet eyes' persuasive powers
Where he meant frost, he scattered flowers.
        Chorus.—By those sweet eyes', etc.

BOTH.

We saw Thee in Thy balmy nest,
Young dawn of our eternal Day!
   We saw Thine eyes break from this East,
And chase the trembling shades away.
   We saw Thee; and we blessed the sight,
We saw Thee by Thine own sweet light.
        Chorus.—We saw Thee, etc.

TITYRUS.

Poor world (said I), what wilt thou do
To entertain this starry Stranger?
   Is this the best thou canst bestow?
A cold, and not too cleanly manger?

Contend, the powers of heaven and earth,
To fit a bed for this huge birth !
   Chorus.—Contend, the powers, etc.

THYRSIS.

Proud world, said I, cease your contest,
And let the mighty Babe alone ;
   The phœnix builds the phœnix' nest,
Love's architecture is its own.
   The Babe whose birth embraves this morn,
   Made His own bed ere He was born.
      Chorus.—The Babe whose birth, etc.

TITYRUS.

I saw the curled drops, soft and slow,
Come hovering o'er the prince's head ;
   Offering Him whitest sheets of snow
To furnish the fair Infant's bed :
   Forbear, said I, be not too bold,
   Your fleece is white, but 'tis too cold.
      Chorus.—Forbear, said I, etc.

THYRSIS.

I saw the obsequious Seraphims
Their rosy fleece of fire bestow,
   For well they now can spare their wing,
Since Heaven itself is here below.
   Well done, said I ; but are you sure
   Your down so warm will pass for pure ?
      Chorus.—Well done, etc.

TITYRUS.

No, no ! your King's not yet to seek
Where to repose His royal head ;
   See, see ! how soon His new-bloomed cheek
'Twixt's mother's breasts is gone to bed.

Sweet choice ! said we : no way but so,
Not to lie cold, yet sleep in snow.
   Chorus.—Sweet choice ! etc.

BOTH.

We saw Thee in Thy balmy nest,
Young dawn of our eternal day !
We saw Thine eyes break from the East,
And chase the trembling shades away.
   We saw Thee ; and we blest the sight,
   We saw Thee by Thine own sweet light.

FULL CHORUS.

Welcome, all wonders in one sight !
Eternity shut in a span !
   Summer in Winter, Day in Night !
Heaven in Earth, and God in man !
     Great, little One ! whose all-embracing birth
     Lifts Earth to Heaven, stoops Heaven to Earth

   Welcome, though not to gold or silk,
To more than Cæsar's birthright is ;
   Two sister seas of virgin-milk,
With many a rarely-tempered kiss,
     That breathes at once both maid and mother,
     Warms in the one, cools in the other.
She sings Thy tears asleep, and dips
   Her kisses in Thy weeping eye ;
She spreads the red leaves of Thy lips,
   That in their buds yet blushing lie :
She 'gainst those mother-diamonds tries
The points of her young eagle's eyes.
Welcome, though not to those gay flies
   Gilded i' th' beams of earthly kings ;
Slippery souls in smiling eyes :
   But to poor shepherds' home-spun things,
       22

Whose wealth's their flock ; whose wit, to be
Well read in their simplicity.
   Yet when young April's husband-showers
Shall bless the fruitful Maia's bed,
   We'll bring the first-born of her flowers
To kiss Thy feet and crown Thy head.
    To Thee, dread Lamb ! whose love must keep
   The shepherds more than they the sheep,
To Thee, meek Majesty ! soft King
   Of simple Graces and sweet Loves,
Each of us his lamb will bring,
   Each his pair of silver doves ;
Till burnt at last in fire of Thy fair eyes,
Ourselves become our own best sacrifice.

Richard Crashaw.

ODE ON THE MORNING OF CHRIST'S NATIVITY.

THIS is the month, and this the happy morn,
Wherein the Son of Heaven's Eternal King,
Of wedded maid and virgin-mother born,
Our great redemption from above did bring ;
For so the holy sages once did sing,
   That He our deadly forfeit should release,
And with His Father work us a perpetual peace.

That glorious form, that light unsufferable,
And that far-beaming blaze of majesty,
Wherewith He wont at Heaven's high council-table
To sit the midst of Trinal Unity,
He laid aside, and here with us to be,
   Forsook the courts of everlasting day,
And chose with us a darksome house of mortal clay.

Say, heavenly Muse, shall not thy sacred vein
Afford a present to the Infant-God?
Hast thou no verse, no hymn, or solemn strain,
To welcome Him to this His new abode,
Now while the heaven, by the sun's team untrod,
   Hath took no print of the approaching light,
And all the spangled host keep watch in squadrons
    bright?

See, how from far, upon the eastern road,
The star-led wizards haste with odours sweet:
O! run, prevent them with thy humble ode,
And lay it lowly at His blessed feet:
Have thou the honour first thy Lord to greet,
   And join thy voice unto the angel-quire,
From out his secret altar touch'd with hallow'd fire.

The Hymn.

It was the winter wild,
While the heaven-born Child
   All meanly wrapt in the rude manger lies;
Nature, in awe to Him,
Had doff'd her gaudy trim,
   With her great Master so to sympathise:
It was no season then for her
To wanton with the sun, her lusty paramour.

Only with speeches fair
She woos the gentle air
   To hide her guilty front with innocent snow:
And on her naked shame,
Pollute with sinful blame,
   The saintly veil of maiden white to throw;
Confounded, that her Maker's eyes
Should look so near upon her foul deformities.

But He, her fears to cease,
Sent down the meek-eyed Peace :
  She, crown'd with olive green, came softly sliding
Down through the turning sphere,
His ready harbinger,
  With turtle wing the amorous clouds dividing ;
And, waving with her myrtle wand,
She strikes a universal peace through sea and land.

No war, or battle's sound,
Was heard the world around :
  The idle spear and shield were high up hung ;
The hookèd chariot stood
Unstain'd with hostile blood ;
  The trumpet spake not to the armèd throng ;
And kings sat still with awful eye,
As if they surely knew their sov'reign Lord was by.

But peaceful was the night,
Wherein the Prince of Light
  His reign of peace upon the earth began ;
The winds, with wonder whist,
Smoothly the waters kiss'd,
  Whispering new joys to the mild ocean,
Who now hath quite forgot to rave,
While birds of calm sit brooding on the charmèd wave.

The stars, with deep amaze,
Stand fix'd in steadfast gaze,
  Bending one way their precious influence :
And will not take their flight,
For all the morning light,
  Or Lucifer that often warn'd them thence ;
But in their glimmering orbs did glow,
Until the Lord himself bespake, and bid them go.

And though the shady gloom
Had given day her room,
   The sun himself withheld his wonted speed,
And hid his head for shame,
As his inferior flame
   The new-enlighten'd world no more should need :
He saw a greater Sun appear
Than his bright throne, or burning axletree, could bear.

The shepherds on the lawn,
Or e'er the point of dawn,
   Sat simply chatting in a rustic row :
Full little thought they then,
That the mighty Pan
   Was kindly come to live with them below ;
Perhaps their loves, or else their sheep,
Was all that did their silly thoughts so busy keep,—

When such music sweet
Their hearts and ears did greet,
   As never was by mortal finger strook ;
Divinely-warbled voice
Answering the stringèd noise,
   As all their souls in blissful rapture took :
The air, such pleasure loth to lose,
With thousand echoes still prolongs each heavenly close.

Nature, that heard such sound,
Beneath the hollow round
   Of Cynthia's seat, the airy region thrilling,
Now was almost won
To think her part was done,
   And that her reign had here its last fulfilling ;
She knew such harmony alone
Could hold all heaven and earth in happier union.

At last surrounds their sight
A globe of circular light,
　　That with long beams the shamefaced night array'd ;
The helmèd cherubim,
And sworded seraphim,
　　Are seen in glittering ranks with wings display'd,
Harping, in loud and solemn quire,
With unexpressive notes, to Heaven's new-born Heir.

Such music (as 'tis said)
Before was never made,
　　But when of old the sons of morning sung,
While the Creator great
His constellations set,
　　And the well-balanced world on hinges hung ;
And cast the dark foundations deep,
And bid the weltering waves their oozy channel keep.

Ring out, ye crystal spheres,
Once bless our human ears,
　　If ye have power to touch our senses so ;
And let your silver chime
Move in melodious time ;
　　And let the bass of heaven's deep organ blow ;
And, with your ninefold harmony,
Make up full concert to the angelic symphony.

For, if such holy song
Enwrap our fancy long,
　　Time will run back and fetch the age of gold ;
And speckled vanity
Will sicken soon and die,
　　And leprous sin will melt from earthly mould ;
And hell itself will pass away,
・ And leave her dolorous mansions to the peering day.

Yea, truth and justice then
Will down return to men,
  Orb'd in a rainbow ; and, like glories wearing,
Mercy will sit between,
Throned in celestial sheen,
  With radiant feet the tissued clouds down steering ;
And heaven, as at some festival,
Will open wide the gates of her high palace hall.

But wisest Fate says No,
This must not yet be so ;
  The Babe yet lies in smiling infancy,
That on the bitter cross
Must redeem our loss,
  So both Himself and us to glorify :
Yet first, to those ychain'd in sleep,   [deep ;
The wakeful trump of doom must thunder through the

With such a horrid clang
As on Mount Sinai rang,
  While the red fire and smouldering clouds out-brake ;
The aged earth, aghast
With terror of that blast,
  Shall from the surface to the centre shake ;
When, at the world's last session,   [throne.
The dreadful Judge in middle air shall spread His

And then at last our bliss
Full and perfect is,
  But now begins ; for, from this happy day,
The old Dragon, under ground
In straiter limits bound,
  Not half so far casts his usurpèd sway ;
And, wroth to see his kingdom fail,
Swinges the scaly horror of his folded tail.

The oracles are dumb,
No voice or hideous hum
 Runs through the archèd roof in words deceiving.
Apollo from his shrine
Can no more divine,
 With hollow shriek the steep of Delphos leaving.
No nightly trance, or breathèd spell,
Inspires the pale-eyed priest from the prophetic cell.

The lonely mountains o'er,
And the resounding shore,
 A voice of weeping heard and loud lament;
From haunted spring and dale,
Edged with poplar pale,
 The parting genius is with sighing sent;
With flower-inwoven tresses torn,   [mourn.
The nymphs in twilight shade of tangled thickets

In consecrated earth,
And on the holy hearth,
 The Lars and Lemures moan with midnight plaint;
In urns, and altars round,
A drear and dying sound
 Affrights the Flamens at their service quaint;
And the chill marble seems to sweat,
While each peculiar power foregoes his wonted seat.

Peor and Baälim
Forsake their temples dim,
 With that twice-batter'd god of Palestine;
And moonèd Ashtaroth,
Heaven's queen and mother both,
 Now sits not girt with tapers' holy shine;
The Lybic Hammon shrinks his horn, [mourn.
In vain the Tyrian maids their wounded Thammuz

And sullen Moloch, fled,
Hath left in shadows dread
  His burning idol all of blackest hue ;
In vain, with cymbals' ring,
They call the grisly king,
  In dismal dance about the furnace blue ;
The brutish gods of Nile as fast,
Isis, and Orus, and the dog Anubis, haste.

Nor is Osiris seen
In Memphian grove or green,
  Trampling the unshower'd grass with lowings loud :
Nor can he be at rest
Within his sacred chest ;
  None but profoundest hell can be his shroud ;
In vain, with timbrell'd anthems dark,
The sable-stolèd sorcerers bear his worshipp'd ark.

He feels from Juda's land
The dreaded Infant's hand,
  The rays of Bethlehem blind his dusky eyn ;
Nor all the gods beside
Longer dare abide,
  Nor Typhon huge ending in snaky twine ;
Our Babe, to show his Godhead true,
Can in his swaddling bands control the damnèd crew.

So, when the sun in bed,
Curtain'd with cloudy red,
  Pillows his chin upon an orient wave,
The flocking shadows pale
Troop to the infernal jail,
  Each fetter'd ghost slips to his several grave ;
And the yellow-skirted fays   [maze.
Fly after the night-steeds, leaving their moon-loved

But see, the Virgin blest
Hath laid her Babe to rest ;
    Time is, our tedious song should here have ending :
Heaven's youngest-teem'd star
Hath fix'd her polish'd car,
    Her sleeping Lord, with handmaid lamp, attending :
And all about the courtly stable
Bright-harness'd angels sit in order serviceable.

John Milton.

ON THE DEATH OF A FAIR INFANT DYING OF A COUGH.

O FAIREST flower, no sooner blown but blasted,
Soft silken primrose fading timelessly,
Summer's chief honour, if thou hadst out-lasted
Bleak winter's force that made thy blossom dry ;
For he, being amorous on that lovely dye
    That did thy cheek envermeil, thought to kiss,
But kill'd, alas ! and then bewail'd his fatal bliss !

For since grim Aquilo, his charioteer,
By boisterous rape the Athenian damsel got,
He thought it touch'd his deity full near,
If likewise he some fair one wedded not,
Thereby to wipe away the infamous blot
    Of long uncoupled bed and childless eld,
Which, 'mongst the wanton gods, a foul reproach was
    held.

So, mounting up in icy-pearlèd car,
Through middle empire of the freezing air,
He wander'd long, till thee he spied from far :
There ended was his quest, there ceased his care :

Down he descended from his snow-soft chair,
  But, all un'wares, with his cold, kind embrace,
Unhoused thy virgin soul from her fair biding-place.

Yet thou art not inglorious in thy fate,
For so Apollo, with unweeting hand,
Whilom did slay his dearly-lovèd mate,
Young Hyacinth, born on Eurotas' strand,
Young Hyacinth, the pride of Spartan land ;
  But then transform'd him to a purple flower :
Alack, that so to change thee Winter had no power !

Yet can I not persuade me thou art dead,
Or that thy corse corrupts in earth's dark womb,
Or that thy beauties lie in wormy bed,
Hid from the world in a low-delvèd tomb ;
Could Heaven, for pity, thee so strictly doom ?
  Oh, no ! for something in thy face did shine
Above mortality, that show'd thou wast divine.

Resolve me, then, O soul most surely blest,
(If so it be that thou these plaints dost hear !)
Tell me, bright spirit, where'er thou hoverest,
Whether above that high first-moving sphere,
Or in the Elysian fields (if such there were) ;
  Oh, say me true, if thou wert mortal wight,
And why from us so quickly thou didst take thy flight?

Wert thou some star which from the ruin'd roof
Of shaked Olympus by mischance didst fall ;
Which careful Jove in nature's true behoof
Took up, and in fit place did reinstal ?
Or did of late Earth's sons besiege the wall
  Of sheeny heaven, and thou, some goddess, fled
Amongst us here below to hide thy nectar'd head?

Or wert thou that just maid, who once before
Forsook the hated earth, oh, tell me sooth,
And camest again to visit us once more?
Or wert thou that sweet-smiling youth?
Or that crown'd matron sage, white-robèd Truth?
　　Or any other of that heavenly brood,
Let down in cloudy throne to do the world some
　　good?

Or wert thou of the golden-wingèd host,
Who, having clad thyself in human weed,
To earth from thy prefixèd seat didst post,
And after short abode fly back with speed,
As if to show what creatures heaven doth breed;
　　Thereby to set the hearts of men on fire,
To scorn the sordid world, and unto heaven aspire?

But oh! why didst thou not stay here below
To bless us with thy heaven-loved innocence,
To slake His wrath whom sin hath made our foe,
To turn swift-rushing black perdition hence?
Or drive away the slaughtering pestilence,
　　To stand 'twixt us and our deservèd smart?
But thou canst best perform that office where thou art.

Then thou, the mother of so sweet a child,
Her false-imagined loss cease to lament,
And wisely learn to curb thy sorrows wild;
Think what a present thou to God hast sent,
And rendered Him with patience what He lent:
　　This if thou do, He will an offspring give,
That till the world's last end shall make thy name to
　　live.

John Milton.

THE RETREAT.

HAPPY those early days, when I
Shined in my angel-infancy !
Before I understood this place
Appointed for my second race,
Or taught my soul to fancy ought
But a white, celestial thought ;
When yet I had not walked above
A mile or two, from my first love,
And looking back—at that short space—
Could see a glimpse of His bright face ;
When on some gilded cloud or flower,
My gazing soul would dwell an hour,
And in those weaker glories spy
Some shadows of eternity ;
Before I taught my tongue to wound
My conscience with a sinful sound,
Or had the black art to dispense
A several sin to every sense,
But felt through all this fleshy dress
Bright shoots of everlastingness.
    O how I long to travel back
And tread again that ancient track !
That I might once more reach that plain
Where first I left my glorious train ;
From whence the enlightened spirit sees
That shady City of palm trees !
But ah ! my soul with too much stay
Is drunk, and staggers in the way !
Some men a forward motion love,
But I by backward steps would move ;
And when this dust falls to the urn,
In that state I came, return.

Henry Vaughan.

CHILDHOOD.

I CANNOT reach it ; and my striving eye
Dazzles at it, as at eternity.
   Were now that chronicle alive,
Those white designs which children drive,
And the thoughts of each harmless hour,
With their content too in my power,
Quickly would I make my path even,
And by mere playing go to heaven.

        Why should men love
A wolf, more than a lamb or dove ?
Or choose hell-fire and brimstone streams
Before bright stars and God's own beams ?
Who kisseth thorns will hurt his face,
But flowers do both refresh and grace,

And sweetly living—fie on men !—
Are, when dead, medicinal then ;
If seeing much shall make staid eyes,
And long experience should make wise,
Since all that age doth teach is ill,
Why should I not love childhood still ?
Why, if I see a rock or shelf,
Shall I from thence cast down myself,
Or, by complying with the world,
From the same precipice be hurled ?
Those observations are but foul
Which make me wise to lose my soul.

And yet the practice worldlings call
Business and weighty actions all,
Checking the poor child for his play,
But gravely cast themselves away.

Dear harmless age ! the short swift span
Where weeping virtue parts with man ;
Where love without lust dwells, and bends
What way we please without self-ends.

An age of mysteries which he
Must live twice that would God's face see ;
Which angels guard, and with it play—
Angels ! which foul men drive away.

How do I study now, and scan
Thee more than e'er I studied man,
And only see through a long night
Thy edges and thy bordering light !
O for thy centre and mid-day !
For sure that is the narrow way !

Henry Vaughan.

TO A CHILD OF QUALITY, FIVE YEARS OLD.

THE AUTHOR THEN FORTY.

Lords, knights, and squires, the numerous band
    That wear the fair Miss Mary's fetters,
Were summoned by her high command,
    To show their passions by their letters.

My pen amongst the rest I took,
    Lest those bright eyes that cannot read
Should dart their kindling fires, and look
    The power they have to be obey'd.

Nor quality, nor reputation
    Forbids me yet my flame to tell,
Dear five-years-old befriends my passion,
    And I may write till she can spell.

For while she makes her silkworms' beds
  With all the tender things I swear;
Whilst all the house my passion reads
  In papers round her baby's hair;

She may receive and own my flame,
  For, though the strictest prudes should know it,
She'll pass for a most virtuous dame,
  And I for an unhappy poet.

Then too, alas! when she shall tear
  The rhymes some younger rival sends;
She'll give me leave to write, I fear,
  And we shall still continue friends.

For, as our different ages move,
  'Tis so ordained (would Fate but mend it!)
That I shall be past making love
  When she begins to comprehend it.
                                Matthew Prior.

A CRADLE SONG.

HUSH! my dear, lie still and slumber;
  Holy angels guard thy bed!
Heavenly blessings without number
  Gently falling on thy head.

Sleep, my babe; thy food and raiment,
  House and home, thy friends provide;
All without thy care and payment
  All thy wants are well supplied.

How much better thou'rt attended
    Than the Son of God could be,
When from Heaven He descended,
    And became a child like thee !

Soft and easy is thy cradle ;
    Coarse and hard thy Saviour lay,
When His birth-place was a stable,
    And His softest bed was hay.

See the kindly shepherds round Him,
    Telling wonders from the sky !
When they sought Him, there they found Him,
    With his Virgin-Mother by.

See the lovely babe a-dressing ;
    Lovely infant, how He smiled !
When He wept, the mother's blessing
    Soothed and hushed the holy child.

Lo, He slumbers in His manger,
    Where the honest oxen fed ;
—Peace, my darling ! here's no danger !
    Here's no ox a-near thy bed !

May'st thou live to know and fear Him,
    Trust and love Him all thy days :
Then go dwell for ever near Him,
    See His face, and sing His praise.

I could give thee thousand kisses
    Hoping what I most desire :
Not a mother's fondest wishes
    Can to greater joys aspire.

Isaac Watts.
23

A SONG UPON MISS HARRIET HANBURY.

Addressed to the Rev. Mr. Birt.

DEAR Doctor of St. Mary's,
In the hundred of 'Bergavenny,
I've seen such a lass
With a shape and a face,
As never was match'd by any.

Such wit, such bloom, and such beauty,
Has this girl of Ponty-Pool, sir,
With eyes that would make
The toughest heart ache,
And the wisest man a fool, sir.

At our fair t'other day she appear'd, sir,
And the Welshmen all flock'd and view'd her ;
And all of them said,
She was fit to have been made
A wife for Owen Tudor.

They would ne'er have been tired of gazing,
And so much her charms did please, sir,
That all of them sat
Till their ale grew flat,
And cold was their toasted cheese, sir.

How happy the lord of the manor,
That shall be of her possest, sir ;
For all must agree
Who my Harriet shall see,
She's a Harriet of the best, sir.

Then pray make a ballad about her ;
We know you have wit if you'd show it,
Then don't be ashamed,
You can never be blamed,—
For a prophet is often a poet !

" But why don't you make one yourself, then ? "
I suppose I by you shall be told, sir !
This beautiful piece
Of Eve's flesh is my niece—
And besides, she's but five years old, sir !

But tho', my dear friend, she's no older,
In her face it may plainly be seen, sir,
That this angel of five,
Will, if she's alive,
Be a goddess at fifteen, sir.

Sir Charles H. Williams.

ON THE BIRTHDAY OF A YOUNG LADY

FOUR YEARS OLD.

OLD creeping time, with silent tread,
Has stol'n four years o'er Molly's head :
The rosebud opens on her cheek,
The meaning eyes begin to speak ;
And in each smiling look is seen
The innocence which plays within.
Nor is the faltering tongue confined
To lisp the dawning of the mind,
But firm and full her words convey
The little all they have to say ;

And each fond parent, as they fall,
Finds volumes in that little all.
    May every charm which now appears
Increase and brighten with her years !
And may that same old creeping time
Go on till she has reached her prime,
Then, like a master of his trade,
Stand still, nor hurt the work he made.

              William Whitehead.

TO A CHILD OF FIVE YEARS OLD.

FAIREST flower, all flowers excelling,
    Which in Milton's page we see ;
Flowers of Eve's embower'd dwelling
    Are, my fair one, types of thee.

Mark, my Polly, how the roses
    Emulate thy damask cheek ;
How the bud its sweets discloses—
    Buds thy opening bloom bespeak.

Lilies are by plain direction,
    Emblems of a double kind :
Emblems of thy fair complexion,
    Emblems of thy fairer mind.

But, dear girl, both flowers and beauty
    Blossom, fade, and die away ;
Then pursue good sense and duty,
    Evergreens, which ne'er decay.

              Nathaniel Cotton.

ON THE RECEIPT OF MY MOTHER'S PICTURE
OUT OF NORFOLK.

Oh that those lips had language! Life has passed
With me but roughly since I heard thee last.
Those lips are thine—thy own sweet smile I see,
The same that oft in childhood solaced me;
Voice only fails, else how distinct they say,
"Grieve not, my child, chase all thy fears away!"
The meek intelligence of those dear eyes
(Blest be the Art that can immortalise,—
The Art that baffles Time's tyrannic claim
To quench it) here shines on me still the same.
    Faithful remembrancer of one so dear,
O welcome guest, though unexpected, here!
Who bidst me honour with an artless song,
Affectionate, a mother lost so long,
I will obey, not willingly alone,
But gladly, as the precept were her own:
And while that face renews my filial grief,
Fancy shall weave a charm for my relief,—
Shall steep me in Elysian reverie,
A momentary dream, that thou art she.
    My mother! when I learned that thou wast dead,
Say, wast thou conscious of the tears I shed?
Hovered thy spirit o'er thy sorrowing son,
Wretch even then, life's journey just begun?
Perhaps thou gav'st me, though unfelt, a kiss;
Perhaps a tear, if souls can weep in bliss—
Ah, that maternal smile! it answers—"Yes."
I heard the bell tolled on thy burial day,
I saw the hearse that bore thee slow away,
And, turning from my nursery window, drew
A long, long sigh, and wept a last adieu!
But was it such?—It was.—Where thou art gone

Adieus and farewells are a sound unknown ;
May I but meet thee on that peaceful shore,
The parting word shall pass my lips no more !
Thy maidens, grieved themselves at my concern,
Oft gave me promise of thy quick return.
What ardently I wished, I long believed,
And, disappointed still, was still deceived ;
By expectation every day beguiled,
Dupe of to-morrow even from a child.
Thus many a sad to-morrow came and went,
Till, all my stock of infant sorrow spent,
I learned at last submission to my lot,
But, though I less deplored thee, ne'er forgot.
    Where once we dwelt our name is heard no more,
Children not thine have trod my nursery floor ;
And where the gardener, Robin, day by day,
Drew me to school along the public way,
Delighted with my bauble coach, and wrapped
In scarlet mantle warm, and velvet capped,
'Tis now become a history little known,
That once we called the pastoral house our own.
Short-lived possession ! but the record fair,
That memory keeps of all thy kindness there,
Still outlives many a storm that has effaced
A thousand other themes less deeply traced.
Thy nightly visits to my chamber made,
That thou mightst know me safe and warmly laid ;
Thy morning bounties ere I left my home,
The biscuit, or confectionary plum ;
The fragrant waters on my cheeks bestowed
By thy own hand, till fresh they shone and glowed :
All this, and more endearing still than all,
Thy constant flow ofl ove, that knew no fall,
Ne'er roughened by those cataracts and breaks,
That humour interposed too often makes ;

And all this legible in Memory's page,
And still to be so to my latest age,
Adds joy to duty, makes me glad to pay
Such honours to thee as my numbers may ;
Perhaps a frail memorial, but sincere,
Not scorned in heaven, though little noticed here.
   Could Time, his flight reversed, restore the hours
When, playing with thy vesture's tissued flowers,
The violet, the pink, and jessamine,
I pricked them into paper with a pin
(And thou wast happier than myself the while,
Wouldst softly speak, and stroke my head, and
    smile),
Could those few pleasant days again appear,
Might one wish bring them, would I wish them here ?
I would not trust my heart—the dear delight
Seems so to be desired, perhaps I might—
But no—what here we call our life is such,
So little to be loved and thou so much,
That I should ill requite thee, to constrain
Thy unbound spirit into bonds again.
   Thou, as a gallant bark from Albion's coast
(The storms all weathered and the ocean crossed)
Shoots into port at some well-havened isle,
Where spices breathe, and brighter seasons smile,
There sits quiescent on the floods that show
Her beauteous form reflected clear below,
While airs impregnated with incense play
Around her, fanning light her streamers gay ;—
So thou, with sails how swift ! hast reached the
    shore,
" Where tempests never beat nor billows roar ;"
And thy loved consort on the dangerous tide
Of life, long since has anchored by thy side.
But me, scarce hoping to attain that rest,

Always from port withheld, always distressed—
Me howling blasts drive devious, tempest-tossed,
Sails ripped, seams opening wide, and compass lost,
And day by day some current's thwarting force
Sets me more distant from a prosperous course.
Yet oh, the thought that thou art safe, and he !
That thought is joy, arrive what may to me.
My boast is not that I deduced my birth
From loins enthroned, and rulers of the earth ;
But higher far my proud pretensions rise—
The son of parents passed into the skies.
And now, Farewell.—Time unrevoked has run
His wonted course, yet what I wished is done.
By Contemplation's help, not sought in vain,
I seem to have lived my childhood o'er again ;
To have renewed the joys that once were mine,
Without the sin of violating thine ;
And while the wings of Fancy still are free,
And I can view this mimic show of thee,
Time has but half succeeded in his theft—
Thyself removed, thy power to soothe me left.

William Cowper.

INTRODUCTION TO "SONGS OF INNOCENCE."

PIPING down the valleys wild,
　Piping songs of pleasant glee,
On a cloud I saw a child,
　And he laughing said to me—

" Pipe a song about a lamb ! "
　So I piped with merry cheer.
" Piper, pipe that song again ; "
　So I piped : he wept to hear.

" Drop thy pipe, thy happy pipe ;
  Sing thy song of happy cheer ! "
So I sang the same again,
  While he wept with joy to hear.

" Piper, sit thee down and write
  In a book that all may read."
So he vanished from my sight ;
  And I plucked a hollow reed,

And I made a rural pen,
  And I stained the water clear,
And I wrote my happy songs
  Every child may joy to hear.

William Blake.

THE LITTLE BLACK BOY.

My mother bore me in the southern wild,
  And I am black, but oh my soul is white !
White as an angel is the English child,
  But I am black, as if bereaved of light.

My mother taught me underneath a tree,
  And, sitting down before the heat of day,
She took me in her lap and kissèd me,
  And, pointing to the East, began to say :

" Look on the rising sun : there God does live,
  And gives his light, and gives his heat away ;
And flowers, and trees, and beasts, and men receive
  Comfort in morning, joy in the noonday.

" And we are put on earth a little space,
    That we may learn to bear the beams of love ;
And these black bodies and this sunburnt face
    Are but a cloud, and like a shady grove.

" For when our souls have learned the heat to bear,
    The cloud will vanish, we shall hear His voice,
Saying, ' Come out from the grove, my love and care,
    And round my golden tent like lambs rejoice.' "

Thus did my mother say, and kissèd me,
    And thus I say to little English boy.
When I from black, and he from white cloud free,
    And round the tent of God like lambs we joy,

I'll shade him from the heat till he can bear
    To lean in joy upon our Father's knee ;
And then I'll stand and stroke his silver hair,
    And be like him, and he will then love me.

William Blake.

HOLY THURSDAY.

'Twas on a Holy Thursday, their innocent faces clean,
Came children walking two and two, in red, and blue,
    and green :
Grey-headed beadles walked before, with wands as white
    as snow,
Till into the high dome of Paul's they like Thames
    waters flow.

Oh what a multitude they seemed, these flowers of
    London town !
Seated in companies they sit, with radiance all their own.

The hum of multitudes was there, but multitudes of
 lambs,
Thousands of little boys and girls raising their innocent
 hands.

Now like a mighty wind they raise to heaven the voice
 of song,
Or like harmonious thunderings the seats of heaven
 among :   [poor,
Beneath them sit the aged men, wise guardians of the
Then cherish pity, lest you drive an angel from your
 door.

William Blake.

INFANT SORROW.

My mother groaned, my father wept :
Into the dangerous world I leapt,
Helpless, naked, piping loud,
Like a fiend hid in a cloud.

Struggling in my father's hands,
Striving against my swaddling-bands,
Bound and weary, I thought best
To sulk upon my mother's breast.

William Blake.

THE LAND OF DREAMS.

Awake, awake, my little boy !
Thou wast thy mother's only joy.
Why dost thou weep in thy gentle sleep ?
Oh wake ! thy father doth thee keep.

" Oh what land is the land of dreams ?
What are its mountains and what are its streams ? "
" Oh father ! I saw my mother there,
Among the lilies by waters fair.

" Among the lambs clothed in white
She walked with her Thomas in sweet delight.
I wept for joy, like a dove I mourn—
Oh when shall I again return ? "

" Dear child ! I also by pleasant streams
Have wandered all night in the land of dreams ;
But, though calm and warm the waters wide,
I could not get to the other side."

" Father, O father ! what do we hear,
In this land of unbelief and fear ?
The land of dreams is better far,
Above the light of the morning-star."

William Blake.

ON THE POET'S DAUGHTER.

HERE lies a rose, a budding rose,
    Blasted before its bloom :
Whose innocence did sweets disclose
    Beyond that flower's perfume.

To those who for her loss are grieved
    This consolation's given—
She's from a world of woe relieved,
    And blooms a rose in Heaven.

Robert Burns.

THE BLIND CHILD.

WHERE's the blind child, so admirably fair,
With guileless dimples, and with flaxen hair
That waves in every breeze ?   He's often seen
Beside yon cottage wall, or on the green,
With others match'd in spirit and in size,
Health on their cheeks, and rapture in their eyes.
That full expanse of voice, to childhood dear,
Soul of their sports, is duly cherish'd here :
And hark ! that laugh is his, that jovial cry ;
He hears the ball and trundling hoop brush by,
And runs the giddy course with all his might,
A very child in everything but sight ;
With circumscribed, but not abated powers—
Play, the great object of his infant hours !
In many a game he takes a noisy part,
And shows the native gladness of his heart ;
But soon he hears, on pleasure all intent,
The new suggestion and the quick assent ;
The grove invites, delight fills every breast—
To leap the ditch, and seek the downy nest.
Away they start ; leave balls and hoops behind,
And one companion leave—the boy is blind !
His fancy paints their distant paths so gay,
That childish fortitude awhile gives way :
He feels the dreadful loss ; yet short the pain,
Soon he resumes his cheerfulness again,
Pondering how best his moments to employ,
He sings his little songs of nameless joy ;
Creeps on the warm green turf for many an hour,
And plucks by chance the white and yellow flower ;
Soothing their stems while resting on his knees,
He binds a nosegay which he never sees ;

Along the homeward path then feels his way,
Lifting his brow against the shining day,
And with a playful rapture round his eyes,
Presents a sighing parent with the prize.

Robert Bloomfield.

THREE YEARS SHE GREW.

THREE years she grew in sun and shower,
Then Nature said, " A lovelier flower
On earth was never sown ;
This child I to myself will take ;
She shall be mine, and I will make
A lady of my own.

" Myself will to my darling be
Both law and impulse : and with me
The girl, in rock and plain,
In earth and heaven, in glade and bower,
Shall feel an overseeing power
To kindle or restrain.

" She shall be sportive as the fawn,
That wild with glee across the lawn
Or up the mountain springs ;
And her's shall be the breathing balm,
And her's the silence and the calm
Of mute insensate things.

" The floating clouds their state shall lend
To her ; for her the willow bend ;
Nor shall she fail to see

Even in the motions of the storm
Grace that shall mould the Maiden's form
By silent sympathy.

" The stars of midnight shall be dear
To her; and she shall lean her ear
In many a secret place,
Where rivulets dance their wayward round,
And beauty born of murmuring sound
Shall pass into her face.

" And vital feelings of delight
Shall rear her form to stately height,
Her virgin bosom swell ;
Such thoughts to Lucy I will give
While she and I together live
Here in this happy dell."

Thus Nature spake—the work was done—
How soon my Lucy's race was run !
She died, and left to me
This heath, this calm, and quiet scene ;
The memory of what has been,
And never more will be.

William Wordsworth.

WE ARE SEVEN.

—A SIMPLE child,
That lightly draws its breath,
And feels its life in every limb,
What should it know of death ?

I met a little cottage girl :
She was eight years old, she said ;
Her hair was thick with many a curl
That clustered round her head.

She had a rustic, woodland air,
And she was wildly clad ;
Her eyes were fair, and very fair ;
—Her beauty made me glad.

"Sisters and brothers, little Maid,
How many may you be?"
"How many? Seven in all," she said,
And wondering looked at me.

"And where are they? I pray you tell."
She answered, "Seven are we ;
And two of us at Conway dwell,
And two are gone to sea.

"Two of us in the churchyard lie,
My sister and my brother ;
And, in the churchyard cottage, I
Dwell near them with my mother."

"You say that two at Conway dwell,
And two are gone to sea,
Yet ye are seven ! I pray you tell,
Sweet Maid, how this may be."

Then did the little maid reply—
"Seven boys and girls are we ;
Two of us in the churchyard lie,
Beneath the churchyard tree."

" You run about, my little Maid,
Your limbs they are alive,
If two are in the churchyard laid,
Then ye are only five."

" Their graves are green, they may be seen,"
The little maid replied,
" Twelve steps or more, from my mother's door
And they are side by side.

" My stockings there I often knit,
My kerchief there I hem ;
And there upon the ground I sit,
And sing a song to them.

" And often after sunset, sir,
When it is light and fair,
I take my little porringer,
And eat my supper there.

" The first that died was sister Jane ;
In bed she moaning lay,
Till God released her from her pain ;
And then she went away.

" So in the churchyard she was laid ;
And, when the grass was dry,
Together round her grave we played,
My brother John and I.

" And when the ground was white with snow,
And I could run and slide,
My brother John was forced to go,
And he lies by her side."

24

" How many are you then," said I,
" If they two are in heaven ? "
Quick was the little Maid's reply,
" O Master ! we are seven."

" But they are dead ; those two are dead !
Their spirits are in heaven ! "
'Twas throwing words away ; for still
The little Maid would have her will,
And said, " Nay, we are seven ! "

William Wordsworth.

LUCY GRAY ; or, SOLITUDE.

Oft I had heard of Lucy Gray :
And, when I crossed the wild,
I chanced to see at break of day
The solitary child.

No mate, no comrade Lucy knew ;
She dwelt on a wild moor,
—The sweetest thing that ever grew
Beside a human door !

You yet may spy the fawn at play,
The hare upon the green ;
But the sweet face of Lucy Gray
Will never more be seen.

" To-night will be a stormy night—
You to the town must go ;
And take a lantern, child, to light
Your mother through the snow."

"That, Father ! will I gladly do :
'Tis scarcely afternoon—
The minster clock has just struck two,
And yonder is the moon ! "

At this the Father raised his hook,
And snapped a faggot band ;
He plied his work ;—and Lucy took
The lantern in her hand.

Not blither is the mountain roe :
With many a wanton stroke
Her feet disperse the powdery snow,
That rises up like smoke.

The storm came on before its time :
She wandered up and down ;
And many a hill did Lucy climb :
But never reached the town.

The wretched parents all that night
Went shouting far and wide ;
But there was neither sound nor sight
To serve them for a guide.

At day-break on a hill they stood
That overlooked the moor ;
And thence they saw the bridge of wood,
A furlong from their door.

They wept—and, turning homeward, cried,
" In heaven we all shall meet ; "
—When in the snow the mother spied
The print of Lucy's feet.

Then downwards from the steep hill's edge
They tracked the footmarks small ;
And through the broken hawthorn hedge,
And by the long stone wall ;

And then an open field they crossed :
The marks were still the same ;
They tracked them on, nor ever lost ;
And to the bridge they came.

They followed from the snowy bank
Those footmarks one by one,
Into the middle of the plank,
And further there were none !

—Yet some maintain that to this day
She is a living child ;
That you may see sweet Lucy Gray
Upon the lonesome wild.

O'er rough and smooth she trips along,
And never looks behind ;
And sings a solitary song
That whistles in the wind.

William Wordsworth.

ODE.

INTIMATIONS OF IMMORTALITY FROM RECOLLECTIONS OF EARLY CHILDHOOD.

" The child is father of the man ;
And I could wish my days to be
Bound each to each by natural piety."

THERE was a time when meadow, grove, and stream,
The earth, and every common sight,
      To me did seem
      Apparelled in celestial light,
The glory and the freshness of a dream.
It is not now as it hath been of yore,—
      Turn wheresoe'er I may,
      By night or day,
The things which I have seen I now can see no more.

      The rainbow comes and goes,
      And lovely is the rose ;
      The moon doth with delight
Look round her when the heavens are bare ;
      Waters on a starry night
      Are beautiful and fair ;
      The sunshine is a glorious birth ;
      But yet I know, where'er I go,
That there hath passed away a glory from the earth.

Now, while the birds thus sing a joyous song,
      And while the young lambs bound
      As to the tabor's sound,
To me alone there came a thought of grief :
A timely utterance gave that thought relief,
      And I again am strong :

The cataracts blow their trumpets from the steep,
No more shall grief of mine the season wrong;
I hear the echoes through the mountains throng,
The winds come to me from the fields of sleep,
     And all the earth is gay;
       Land and sea
   Give themselves up to jollity,
     And with the heart of May
  Doth every beast keep holiday;—
     Thou child of joy,
Shout round me, let me hear thy shouts, thou happy
     shepherd boy!

Ye blessed creatures, I have heard the call
     Ye to each other make; I see
The heavens laugh with you in your jubilee;
    My heart is at your festival,
     My head hath its coronal,
The fulness of your bliss, I feel—I feel it all.
     O evil day! if I were sullen
     While the earth itself is adorning,
      The sweet May morning,
    And the children are pulling,
      On every side,
    In a thousand valleys far and wide,
    Fresh flowers; while the sun shines warm,
And the babe leaps up on his mother's arm:—
    I hear, I hear, with joy I hear!
    But there's a tree, of many, one
A single field which I have looked upon,
Both of them speak of something that is gone:
     The pansy at my feet
     Doth the same tale repeat:
Whither is fled the visionary gleam?
Where is it now, the glory and the dream?

Our birth is but a sleep and a forgetting:
The soul that rises with us, our life's star,
    Hath had elsewhere its setting,
      And cometh from afar:
    Not in entire forgetfulness,
    And not in utter nakedness,
But trailing clouds of glory do we come
    From God, who is our home:
Heaven lies about us in our infancy!
Shades of the prison-house begin to close
    Upon the growing boy,
But he beholds the light, and whence it flows,
    He sees it in his joy;
The youth, who daily farther from the east
    Must travel, still is nature's priest,
    And by the vision splendid
    Is on his way attended;
At length the man perceives it die away,
And fade into the light of common day.

Earth fills her lap with pleasures of her own;
Yearnings she hath in her own natural kind,
And, even with something of a mother's mind,
    And no unworthy aim,
    The homely nurse doth all she can
To make her foster-child, her inmate man,
    Forget the glories he hath known,
And that imperial palace whence he came.
Behold the child among his new-born blisses,
A six-years' darling of a pigmy size!
See where 'mid work of his own hand he lies,
Fretted by sallies of his mother's kisses,
With light upon him from his father's eyes!
See, at his feet, some little plan or chart,
Some fragment from his dream of human life,

Shaped by himself with newly-learnèd art;
   A wedding or a festival,
   A mourning or a funeral;
      And this hath now his heart,
      And unto this he frames his song:
      Then will he fit his tongue
To dialogues of business, love, or strife;
     But it will not be long
     Ere this be thrown aside,
     And with new joy and pride
The little actor cons another part;
Filling from time to time his "humorous stage"
With all the persons, down to palsied age,
That life brings with her in her equipage;
     As if his whole vocation
     Were endless imitation.

Thou, whose exterior semblance doth belie
     Thy soul's immensity;
Thou best philosopher, who yet dost keep
Thy heritage, thou eye among the blind,
That, deaf and silent, read'st the eternal deep,
Haunted for ever by the eternal mind—
     Mighty prophet! seer blest!
     On whom those truths do rest,
Which we are toiling all our lives to find,
In darkness lost, the darkness of the grave;
Thou, over whom thy immortality
Broods like the day, a master o'er a slave,
A presence which is not to be put by;
Thou little child, yet glorious in the might
Of heaven-born freedom on thy being's height,
Why with such earnest pains dost thou provoke
The years to bring the inevitable yoke,
Thus blindly with thy blessedness at strife?

Full soon thy soul shall have her earthly freight,
And custom lie upon thee with a weight,
Heavy as frost, and deep almost as life !

O joy ! that in our embers
Is something that doth live,
That nature yet remembers
What was so fugitive !
The thought of our past years in me doth breed
Perpetual benediction : not indeed
For that which is most worthy to be blest ;
Delight and liberty, the simple creed
Of childhood, whether busy or at rest,
With new-fledged hope still fluttering in his breast :
Not for these I raise
The song of thanks and praise ;
But for those obstinate questionings
Of sense and outward things,
Fallings from us, vanishings ;
Blank misgivings of a creature
Moving about in worlds not realised,
High instincts before which our mortal nature
Did tremble like a guilty thing surprised :
But for those first affections,
Those shadowy recollections,
Which, be they what they may,
Are yet the fountain light of all our day,
Are yet a master light of all our seeing ;
Uphold us, cherish, and have power to make
Our noisy years seem moments in the being
Of the eternal silence : truths that wake
To perish never ;
Which neither listlessness, nor mad endeavour,
Nor man nor boy,
Nor all that is at enmity with joy,

Can utterly abolish or destroy !
  Hence, in a season of calm weather,
   Though inland far we be,
Our souls have sight of that immortal sea
  Which brought us hither,
   Can in a moment travel thither,
And see the children sport upon the shore,
And hear the mighty waters rolling evermore.

Then sing, ye birds, sing, sing a joyous song !
   And let the young lambs bound
   As to the tabor's sound !
We in thought will join your throng,
   Ye that pipe and ye that play,
   Ye that through your hearts to-day
   Feel the gladness of the May !
What though the radiance which was once so bright
Be now for ever taken from my sight,
  Though nothing can bring back the hour
Of splendour in the grass, of glory in the flower ;
   We will grieve not, rather find
   Strength in what remains behind ;
   In the primal sympathy
   Which having been must ever be,
   In the soothing thoughts that spring
   Out of human suffering,
   In the faith that looks through death,
In years that bring the philosophic mind.

And O ye fountains, meadows, hills, and groves,
Think not of any severing of our loves !
Yet in my heart of hearts I feel your might :
I only have relinquished one delight
To live beneath your more habitual sway.
I love the brooks which down their channels fret,

Even more than when I tripped lightly as they;
The innocent brightness of a new-born day
             Is lovely yet;
The clouds that gather round the setting sun
Do take a sober colouring from an eye
That hath kept watch o'er man's mortality;
Another race hath been, and other palms are won.
Thanks to the human heart by which we live,
Thanks to its tenderness, its joys, and fears,
To me the meanest flower that blows can give
Thoughts that do often lie too deep for tears.
                    William Wordsworth.

———

LULLABY OF AN INFANT CHIEF.

O, HUSH thee, my babie, thy sire was a knight,
Thy mother a lady, both lovely and bright;
The woods and the glens, from the towers which we see,
They all are belonging, dear babie, to thee.
             O ho ro, i ri ri, cadul gu lo,
             O ho ro, i ri ri.

O, fear not the bugle, though loudly it blows,
It calls but the warders that guard thy repose;
Their bows would be bended, their blades would be red
Ere the step of a foeman draws near to thy bed.
             O ho ro, i ri ri, etc.

O, hush thee, my babie, the time will soon come
When thy sleep shall be broken by trumpet and drum;
Then hush thee, my darling, take rest while you may,
For strife comes with manhood, and waking with day.
             O ho ro, i ri ri, etc.
                    Sir Walter Scott.

EPITAPH ON AN INFANT.

Its balmy life the infant blest,
Relaxing from its mother's breast ;
How sweet it heaves the happy sigh
Of innocent satiety !

And such my infant's latest sigh !
O tell, rude stone, the passer by,
That here the pretty babe doth lie
Death sang to sleep with lullaby.

Samuel Taylor Coleridge.

TO AN INFANT.

Ah ! cease thy tears and sobs, my little Life !
I did but snatch away the unclasped knife :
Some safer toy will soon arrest thine eye,
And to quick laughter change this peevish cry !
Poor stumbler on the rocky coast of woe,
Tutored by pain each source of pain to know !
Alike the foodful fruit and scorching fire
Awake thy eager grasp and young desire ;
Alike the Good, the Ill offend thy sight,
And rouse the stormy sense of shrill affright !
Untaught, yet wise, 'mid all thy brief alarms
Thou closely clingest to thy Mother's arms,
Nestling thy little face in that fond breast
Whose anxious heavings lull thee to thy rest !
Man's breathing Miniature ! thou mak'st me sigh—
A Babe art thou—and such a thing am I !
To anger rapid and as soon appeased,
For trifles mourning and by trifles pleased,

Break Friendship's mirror with a tetchy blow,
Yet snatch what coals of fire on Pleasure's altar
   glow !

O thou that rearest with celestial aim,
The future Seraph in my mortal frame,
Thrice holy Faith ! whatever thorns I meet,
As on I totter with unpractised feet,
Still let me stretch my arms and cling to thee,
Meek nurse of souls through their long infancy !

Samuel Taylor Coleridge.

THE LAST CRADLE SONG.

BAWLOO, my bonnie baby, bawlililu,
   Light be thy care and cumber ;
Bawloo, my bonnie baby, bawlililu,
   Oh, sweet be thy sinless slumber.
Ere thou wert born, my youthful heart
   Yearned o'er my babe with sorrow ;
Long is the night noon that we must part,
   But bright shall arise the morrow.

Bawloo, my bonnie baby, bawlililu,
   Here no more shall I see thee ;
Bawloo, my bonnie baby, bawlililu,
   O, sair is my heart to lea' thee ?
But far within yon sky so blue,
   In love that fail shall never,
In valleys beyond the land of the dew,
   I'll sing to my baby for ever.

James Hogg.

QUEEN MARY'S CHRISTENING.

THE first wish of Queen Mary's heart
    Is that she may bear a son,
Who shall inherit in his time
    The kingdom of Aragon.

She hath put up prayers to all the Saints
    This blessing to accord,
But chiefly she hath called upon
    The Apostles of our Lord.

The second wish of Queen Mary's heart
    Is to have that son called James,
Because she thought for a Spanish king
    'Twas the best of all good names.

To give him this name of her own will
    Is what may not be done ;
For, having applied to all the Twelve,
    She may not prefer the one.

By one of their names she had vowed to call
    Her son, if son it should be ;
But which is a point whereon she must let
    The Apostles themselves agree.

Already Queen Mary hath to them
    Contracted a grateful debt ;
And from their patronage she hoped
    For these further blessings yet.

Alas ! it was not her hap to be
    As handsome as she was good ;
And that her husband King Pedro thought so,
    She very well understood.

She had lost him from her lawful bed
    For lack of personal graces ;
And by prayers to them, and a pious deceit,
    She had compassed his embraces.

But, if this hope of a son should fail,
    All hope must fail with it then ;
For she could not expect by a second device
    To compass the king again.

Queen Mary hath had her first heart's wish—
    She hath brought forth a beautiful boy ;
And the bells have rung, and masses been sung,
    And bonfires have blazed for joy.

And many's the cask of the good red wine,
    And many the cask of the white,
Which was broached for joy that morning,
    And emptied before it was night.

But now for Queen Mary's second heart's wish,
    It must be determined now ;
And Bishop Boyl, her confessor,
    Is the person who taught her how.

Twelve waxen tapers he hath made,
    In size and weight the same ;
And to each of these twelve tapers
    He hath given an Apostle's name.

One holy Nun had bleached the wax,
    Another the wicks had spun ;
And the golden candlesticks were blest
    Which they were set upon.

From that which should burn the longest,
   The infant his name must take ;
And the saint who owned it was to be
   His patron for his name's sake.

A godlier or a goodlier sight
   Was nowhere to be secn,
Methinks, that day in Christendom,
   Than in the chamber of that good Queen.

Twelve little altars have been there
   Erected, for the nonce ;
And the twelve tapers are set thereon,
   Which are all to be lit at once.

Altars more gorgeously dressed
   You nowhere could desire ;
At each there stood a ministering Priest,
   In his most rich attire.

A high altar hath there been raised,
   Where the crucifix you see ;
And the sacred pyx that shines with gold,
   And sparkles with jewelry.

Bishop Boyl, with his precious mitre on,
   Hath taken there his stand,
In robes which were embroidered
   By the Queen's own royal hand.

In one part of the ante-room,
   The ladies of the Queen,
All with their rosaries in hand,
   Upon their knees are seen.

In the other part of the ante-room,
   The chiefs of the realm you behold,
Ricos Omes, and Bishops and Abbots,
   And Knights and Barons bold.

Queen Mary could behold all this
   As she lay in her state bed ;
And from the pillow needed not
   To lift her languid head.

One fear she had, though still her heart
   The unwelcome thought eschewed,
That haply the unlucky lot
   Might fall upon St. Jude.

But the saints, she trusted, that ill chance
   Would certainly forefend ;
And moreover there was a double hope
   Of seeing the wished-for end ;

Because there was a double chance
   For the best of all good names :
If it should nor be Santiago himself,
   It might be the lesser St. James.

And now Bishop Boyl hath said the mass ;
   And as soon as the mass was done,
The priests, who by the twelve tapers stood,
   Each instantly lighted one.

The tapers were short, and slender too ;
   Yet to the expectant throng,
Before they to the socket burnt,
   The time, I trow, seemed long.

The first that went out was St. Peter,
  The second was St. John ;
And now St. Matthias is going,
  And now St. Matthew is gone.

Next there went St. Andrew ;
  There goes St. Philip too ;
And, see ! there is an end
  Of St. Bartholomew.

St. Simon is in the snuff;
  But it was a matter of doubt
Whether he or St. Thomas could be said
  Soonest to have gone out.

There are only three remaining—
  St. Jude and the two Saints James ;
And great was then Queen Mary's hope
  For the best of all good names.

Great was then Queen Mary's hope ;
  But greater her fear, I guess,
When one of the three went out,
  And that one was St. James the less.

They are now within less than quarter-inch,
  The only remaining two !
When there came a thief in St. James,
  And it made a gutter too !

Up started Queen Mary ;
  Up she sate in her bed :
" I never can call him Judas ! "
  She clasped her hands and said.

" I never can call him Judas,"
   Again did she exclaim :
" Holy Mother, preserve us !
   It is not a Christian name ! "

She spread her hands, and clasped them again,
   And the infant in the cradle
Set up a cry, an angry cry,
   As loud as he was able.

" Holy Mother, preserve us ! "
   The Queen her prayer renewed ;
When in came a moth at the window
   And fluttered about St. Jude.

St. James had fallen in his socket,
   But as yet the flame is not out ;
And St. Jude had singed the silly moth
   That flutters so blindly about.

And before the flame and the molten wax
   That silly moth could kill,
It hath beat out St. Jude with its wings,
   And St. James is burning still !

Oh, that was a joy for Queen Mary's heart !
   The babe is christened James:
The Prince of Aragon hath got
   The best of all good names !

Glory to Santiago,
   The mighty one in war !
James he is called, and he shall be
   King James the Conqueror !

Now shall the Crescent wane,
  The Cross he set on high
In triumph upon many a mosque ;
  Woe, woe, to Mahometry !

Valencia shall be subdued ;
  Majorca shall be won ;
The Moors be routed everywhere ;
  Joy, joy for Aragon !

Shine brighter now, ye stars, that crown
  Our Lady del Pilar !
And rejoice in thy grave, Cid Campeador,
  Ruy Diez de Bivar !

                              Robert Southey.

ROSINA.

ROSINA ran down Prior Park,
Joyous and buoyant as a lark,
The little girl, light-heel'd, light-hearted,
Challenged me ; and away we started.
Soon in a flutter she return'd,
And cheek, and brow, and bosom burn'd.
She fairly owns my full success
In catching her—she could no less,
And said to her mamma, who smiled
Yet lovelier on her lovely child,
" You cannot think how fast he ran
For such a very old, old man !
He wouldn't kiss me when he might,
And, catching me, he had a right ;
Such modesty I never knew—
He would no more kiss me than you ! "

                              Walter Savage Landor.

BEFORE A SAINT'S PICTURE.

MY serious son ! I see thee look
First on the picture, then the book.
I catch the wish that thou couldst paint
The yearnings of the ecstatic saint.
Give it not up, my serious son !
Wish it again, and it is done.
Seldom will any fail who tries
With patient hand and steadfast eyes,
And woos the true with such pure sighs.

Walter Savage Landor.

DIFFERENT GRACES.

AROUND the child bend all the three
Sweet Graces—Faith, Hope, Charity.
Around the man bend other faces—
Pride, Envy, Malice, are his Graces.

Walter Savage Landor.

CHILDREN PLAYING IN A CHURCHYARD.

CHILDREN, keep up that harmless play ;
Your kinder angels plainly say,
By God's authority, ye may.

Be prompt His holy word to hear,
It teaches you to banish fear :
The lesson lies on all sides near.

Ten summers hence the spriteliest lad,
In Nature's face will look more sad,
And ask where are those smiles she had.

Ere many days the last will close . . .
Play on, play on ; for then (who knows?)
He who plays here may here repose.

Walter Savage Landor.

THERE ARE SOME WISHES.

THERE are some wishes that may start,
Nor cloud the brow nor sting the heart,
Gladly then would I see how smiled
One who now fondles with her child ;
How smiled she but six years ago,
Herself a child, or nearly so.
Yes, let me bring before my sight
The silken tresses chain'd up tight,
The tiny fingers tipt with red
By tossing up the strawberry-bed ;
Half-open lips, long violet eyes,
A little rounder with surprise,
And then (her chin against her knee),
"Mamma ! who can that stranger be ?
How grave the smile he smiles on me !"

Walter Savage Landor.

CHILD OF A DAY.

CHILD of a day, thou knowest not
   The tears that overflow thine urn,
The gushing eyes that read thy lot,
  ·Nor, if thou knewest, could'st return !

And why the wish ! the pure and blest
   Watch like thy mother o'er thy sleep.
O peaceful night ! O envied rest !
   Thou wilt not ever see her weep.

Walter Savage Landor.

CHILDHOOD.

IN my poor mind it is most sweet to muse
Upon the days gone by ; to act in thought
Past seasons o'er, and be again a child ;
To sit in fancy on the turf-clad slope   [flowers,
Down which the child would roll ; to pluck gay
Make posies in the sun, which the child's hand
(Childhood offended soon, soon reconciled)
Would throw away, and straight take up again,
Then fling them to the winds, and o'er the lawn
Bound with so playful and so light a foot,
That the pressed daisy scarce declined her head.

Charles Lamb.

FEIGNED COURAGE.

HORATIO, of ideal courage vain,
Was flourishing in air his father's cane,
And, as the fumes of valour swelled his pate,
Now thought himself *this* hero, and now *that* ;

"And now," he cried, "I will Achilles be;
My sword I brandish, see, the Trojans flee.
Now I'll be Hector when his angry blade
A lane through heaps of slaughtered Grecians made!
And now by deeds still braver I'll convince,
I am no less than Edward the Black Prince.
Give way, ye coward French!" As thus he spoke,
And aimed in fancy a sufficient stroke
To fix the fate of Cressy or Poictiers
(The nurse relates the hero's fate with tears);
He struck his milk-white hand against a nail,
Sees his own blood, and feels his courage fail.
Ah! where is now that boasted valour flown,
That in the tented field so late was shown?
Achilles weeps, great Hector hangs his head!
And the Black Prince goes whimpering to bed.

Mary Lamb.

PARENTAL RECOLLECTIONS.

A CHILD's a plaything for an hour:
   Its pretty tricks we try
For that, or for a longer space;
   Then tire and lay it by.

But I knew one that to itself
   All reasons would control;
That would have mocked the sense of pain
   Out of a grievèd soul.

Thou struggler into loving arms,
   Young climber up of knees!
When I forget thy thousand ways,
   Then life and all shall cease.

Mary Lamb.

THE NEW-BORN INFANT.

WHETHER beneath sweet beds of roses,
As foolish little Ann supposes,
The spirit of a babe reposes
　　Before it to the body come ;
Or, as philosophy more wise
Thinks, it descendeth from the skies,
　　We know the babe's now in the room.

And that is all which is quite clear
Even to philosophy, my dear.
　　The God that made us can alone
Reveal from whence a spirit's brought
Into young life, to light, and thought ;
　　And this the wisest man must own.

We'll talk now of the babe's surprise
When first he opens his new eyes,
　　And first receives delicious food.
Before the age of six or seven,
To mortal children is not given
　　Much reason, else I think he would

(And very naturally) wonder
What happy star he was born under,
　　That he should be the only care
Of the dear, sweet, food-giving lady,
Who fondly calls him her own baby,
　　Her darling hope, her infant heir.

Mary Lamb.

TO T. L. H.,

SIX YEARS OLD, DURING A SICKNESS.

SLEEP breathes at last from out thee,
　My little, patient boy;
And balmy rest about thee
　Smooths off the day's annoy.
　　I sit me down, and think
　　Of all thy winning ways;
Yet almost wish, with sudden shrink,
　That I had less to praise.

Thy sidelong pillowed meekness,
　Thy thanks to all that aid,
Thy heart, in pain and weakness,
　Of fancied faults afraid;
　　The little trembling hand
　　That wipes thy quiet tears,—
These, these are things that may demand
　Dread memories for years.

Sorrows I've had, severe ones,
　I will not think of now;
And calmly, midst my dear ones,
　Have wasted with dry brow;
　　But when thy fingers press
　　And pat my stooping head,
I cannot bear the gentleness,—
　The tears are in their bed.

Ah, first-born of thy mother,
　When life and hope were new,
Kind playmate of thy brother,
　Thy sister, father too;

My light, where'er I go,
  My bird, when prison-bound,
My hand in hand companion,—no,
  My prayers shall hold thee round.

To say " He has departed "—
  " His voice "—" his face "—is gone;
To feel impatient-hearted,
  Yet feel we must bear on ;
    Ah, I could not endure
    To whisper of such woe,
Unless I felt this sleep ensure
  That it will not be so.

Yes, still he's fixed and sleeping !
  This silence too the while—
Its very hush and creeping
  Seem whispering us a smile:
    Something divine and dim
    Seems going by one's ear,
Like parting wings of Cherubim,
  Who say, " We've finished here."

                    Leigh Hunt.

GOLDEN-TRESSED ADELAIDE.

Sing, I pray, a little song,
    Mother dear !
Neither sad nor very long:
It is for a little maid,
Golden-tressèd Adelaide !
Therefore let it suit a merry, merry ear,
    Mother dear !

Let it be a merry strain,
    Mother dear !
Shunning e'en the thought of pain :
For our gentle child will weep,
If the theme be dark and deep ;
And *we* will not draw a single tear,
    Mother dear !

Childhood shall be all divine,
    Mother dear !
And like endless summer shine :
Gay as Edward's shouts and cries,
Bright as Agnes' azure eyes ;
Therefore let thy song be merry : dost thou hear,
    Mother dear ?

    Byran Waller Procter (Barry Cornwall).

TO WILLIAM SHELLEY.

THE billows on the beach are leaping around it,
The bark is weak and frail,
The sea looks black, and the clouds that bound it,
Darkly strew the gale.
Come with me, thou delightful child,
Come with me, though the wave is wild,
And the winds are loose, we must not stay,
Or the slaves of the law may rend thee away.

They have taken thy brother and sister dear,
They have made them unfit for thee ;
They have withered the smile and dried the tear
Which should have been sacred to me.

To a blighting faith and a cause of crime
They have bound them slaves in youthly prime,
And they will curse my name and thee
Because we are fearless and free.

Come thou, belovèd as thou art;
Another sleepeth still
Near thy sweet mother's anxious heart,
Which thou with joy shalt fill,
With fairest smiles of wonder thrown
On that which is indeed our own,
And which in distant lands will be
The dearest playmate unto thee.

Fear not the tyrants will rule for ever,
Or the priests of the evil faith;
They stand on the brink of that raging river,
Whose waves they have tainted with death.
It is fed from the depth of a thousand dells,
Around them it foams, and rages, and swells;
And their swords and their sceptres I floating see,
Like wrecks on the surge of eternity.

Rest, rest, and shriek not, thou gentle child!
The rocking of the boat thou fearest,
And the cold spray and the clamour wild?—
There sit between us two, those dearest—
Me and thy mother—well we know
The storm at which thou tremblest so,
With all its dark and hungry graves,
Less cruel than the savage slaves
Who hunt us o'er these sheltering waves.

This hour will in thy memory
Be a dream of days forgotten long;

We soon shall dwell by the azure sea
Of serene and golden Italy,
Or Greece, the mother of the free ;
And I will teach thine infant tongue
To call upon those heroes old
In their own language, and will mould
Thy growing spirit in the flame
Of Grecian lore, that by such name
A patriot's birthright thou mayst claim !

Percy Bysshe Shelley.

CASABIANCA.*

THE boy stood on the burning deck
  Whence all but he had fled ;
The flame that lit the battle's wreck
  Shone round him o'er his head.

Yet beautiful and bright he stood,
  As born to rule the storm—
A creature of heroic blood,
  A proud, though child-like form.

The flames rolled on—he would not go
  Without his father's word ;
That father, faint in death below,
  His voice no longer heard.

* Young Casabianca, a boy about thirteen years old, son of the
Admiral of the Orient, remained at his post (in the battle of the
Nile) after the ship had taken fire, and all the guns had been
abandoned ; and perished in the explosion of the vessel, when
the flames had reached the powder.

He called aloud :—" Say, father, say,
  If yet my task is done ! "
He knew not that the chieftain lay
  Unconscious of his son.

" Speak, father ! " once again he cried,
  " If I may yet be gone ! "
And but the booming shots replied,
  And fast the flames rolled on.

Upon his brow he felt their breath,
  And in his waving hair,
And looked from that lone post of death
  In still yet brave despair.

And shouted but once more aloud,
  " My father ! must I stay ? "
While o'er him fast, through sail and shroud,
  The wreathing fires made way.

They wrapt the ship in splendour wild,
  They caught the flag on high,
And streamed above the gallant child
  Like banners in the sky.

There came a burst of thunder-sound—
  The boy—oh ! where was he ?
Ask of the winds that far around
  With fragments strewed the sea !—

With mast and helm, and pennon fair,
  That well had borne their part ;
But the noblest thing which perished there
  Was that young faithful heart !

Felicia Hemans.

THE CHILD'S LAST SLEEP.

SUGGESTED BY A MONUMENT OF CHANTREY'S.

Thou sleepest—but when wilt thou wake, fair child?
When the fawn awakes in the forest wild?
When the lark's wing mounts with the breeze of morn?
When the first rich breath of the rose is born?—
Lonely thou sleepest! yet something lies
Too deep and still on thy soft-sealed eyes;
Mournful, though sweet, is thy rest to see—
When will the hour of thy rising be?

Not when the fawn wakes—not when the lark
On the crimson cloud of the morn floats dark.
Grief with vain passionate tears hath wet
The hair, shedding gleams from thy pale brow yet;
Love, with sad kisses unfelt, hath pressed
Thy meek-dropt eyelids and quiet breast;
And the glad spring, calling out bird and bee,
Shall colour all blossoms, fair child! but thee.

Thou'rt gone from us, bright one!—that *thou* should'st
    die,
And life be left to the butterfly! *
Thou'rt gone as a dewdrop is swept from the bough:
Oh! for the world where thy home is now!
How may we love but in doubt and fear,
How may we anchor our fond hearts here;
How should e'en joy but a trembler be,
Beautiful dust! when we look on thee.

                              Felicia Hemans.

* A butterfly, as if resting on a flower, is sculptured on the
monument.

THE SABBATH DAY'S CHILD.

PURE, precious drop of dear mortality,
Untainted fount of life's meandering stream,
Whose innocence is like the dewy beam
Of morn, a visible reality,
Holy and quiet as a hermit's dream :
Unconscious witness to the promised birth
Of perfect good, that may not grow on earth,
Nor be computed by the worldly worth
And stated limits of morality ;
Fair type and pledge of full redemption given,
Through Him that saith, 'Of such is the kingdom of heaven!'

Sweet infant, whom thy brooding parents love
For what thou art, and what they hope to see thee,
Unhallow'd sprites and earth-born phantoms flee thee ;
Thy soft simplicity, a hovering dove,
That still keeps watch from blight and bane to free thee,
With its weak wings, in peaceful care outspread,
Fanning invisibly thy pillow'd head,
Strikes evil powers with reverential dread,
Beyond the sulphurous bolts of fabled Jove,
Or whatsoe'er of amulet or charm
Fond Ignorance devised to save poor souls from harm.

To see thee sleeping on thy mother's breast,
It were indeed a lovely sight to see—
Who would believe that restless sin can be
In the same world that holds such sinless rest ?
Happy art thou, sweet babe, and happy she
Whose voice alone can still thy baby cries,
Now still itself ; yet pensive smiles, and sighs,
And the mute meanings of a mother's eyes
Declare her thinking, deep felicity :

26

A bliss, my babe, how much unlike to thine,
Mingled with earthly fears, yet cheer'd with hope divine.

Thou breathing image of the life of Nature !
Say rather, image of a happy death—
For the vicissitudes of vital breath,
Of all infirmity the slave and creature,
That by the act of being perisheth,
Are far unlike that slumber's perfect peace
Which seems too absolute and pure to cease,
Or suffer diminution, or increase,
Or change of hue, proportion, shape, or feature ;
A calm, it seems, that is not, shall not be,
Save in the silent depths of calm eternity.

A star reflected in a dimpling rill
That moves as slow it hardly moves at all ;
The shadow of a white-robed waterfall
Seen in the lake beneath when all is still ;
A wandering cloud, that with its fleecy pall
Whitens the lustre of an autumn moon ;
A sudden breeze that cools the cheek of noon,
Not mark'd till miss'd—so soft it fades, and soon—
Whatever else the fond inventive skill
Of fancy may suggest cannot apply
Fit semblance of the sleeping life of infancy.

Calm art thou as the blessed Sabbath eve,
The blessed Sabbath eve when thou wast born ;
Yet sprightly as a summer Sabbath morn,
When surely 'twere a thing unmeet to grieve :
When ribbons gay the village maids adorn,
And Sabbath music, on the swelling gales,
Floats to the farthest nooks of winding vales,
And summons all the beauty of the dales.

Fit music this a stranger to receive,
And, lovely child, it rang to welcome thee,
Announcing thy approach with gladsome minstrelsy.

So be thy life—a gentle Sabbath, pure
From worthless strivings of the work-day earth :
May time make good the omen of thy birth,
Nor worldly care thy growing thoughts immure,
Nor hard-eyed thrift usurp the throne of mirth
On thy smooth brow.   And though fast coming years
Must bring their fated dower of maiden fears,
Of timid blushes, sighs, and fertile tears,
Soft sorrow's sweetest offspring, and her cure ;
May every day of thine be good and holy,
And thy worst woe a pensive Sabbath melancholy.

Hartley Coleridge.

CHILDHOOD.

OH what a wilderness were this sad world
If man were always man, and never child ;
If Nature gave no time, so sweetly wild,
When every thought is deftly crisped and curled,
Like fragrant hyacinth with dew impearled,
And every feeling in itself confiding,
Yet never single, but continuous, gliding
With wavy motion as, on wings unfurled,
A seraph clips Empyreal !   Such man was
Ere sin had made him know himself too well.
No child was born ere that primeval loss.
What might have been no living soul can tell :
But Heaven is kind, and therefore all possess
Once in their life fair Eden's simpleness.

Hartley Coleridge.

"OF SUCH IS THE KINGDOM OF GOD."

IN stature perfect, and in every gift
Which God would on His favourite work bestow,
Did our great Parent his pure form uplift,
And sprang from earth, the Lord of all below.

But Adam fell before a child was born,
And want and weakness with his fall began;
So his first offspring was a thing forlorn,
In human shape, without the strength of man:

So, Heaven has doomed that all of Adam's race,
Naked and helpless, shall their course begin—
E'en at their birth confess their need of grace—
And weeping, wail the penalty of sin.

Yet sure the babe is in the cradle blest,
Since God Himself a baby deign'd to be—
And slept upon a mortal mother's breast,
And steep'd in baby tears—His Deity.

O sleep, sweet infant, for we all must sleep—
And wake like babes, that we may wake with Him,
Who watches still His own from harm to keep,
And o'er them spreads the wings of cherubim.

Hartley Coleridge.

A PARENTAL ODE TO MY SON,

AGED THREE YEARS AND FIVE MONTHS.

THOU happy, happy elf!
(But stop,—first let me kiss away that tear)—
Thou tiny image of myself!
(My love, he's poking peas into his ear!)
Thou merry laughing sprite!
With spirits feather-light,
Untouch'd by sorrow, and unsoil'd by sin—
(Good heavens! the child is swallowing a pin!)
Thou little trickey Puck!
With antic toys so funnily bestuck,
Light as the singing bird that wings the air—
(The door! the door! he'll tumble down the stair!)
Thou darling of thy sire!
(Why, Janet, he'll set his pinafore a-fire!)
Thou imp of mirth and joy!
In love's dear chain so strong and bright a link,
Thou idol of thy parents—(Drat the boy!
There goes my ink!)

Thou cherub—but of earth;
Fit playfellow for Fays, by moonlight pale,
In harmless sport and mirth,
(That dog will bite him if he pulls its tail!)
Thou human humming-bee, extracting honey
From ev'ry blossom in the world that blows,
Singing in Youth's Elysium ever sunny,
(Another tumble!—that's his precious nose!)

Thy father's pride and hope !
(He'll break the mirror with that skipping-rope !)
With pure heart newly stamp'd from Nature's mint,
(Where *did* he learn that squint ?)

The young domestic dove !
(He'll have that jug off, with another shove !)
Dear nursling of the hymeneal nest !
(Are those torn clothes his best ?)
Little epitome of man !
(He'll climb upon the table, that's his plan !)
Touched with the beauteous tints of dawning life—
(He's got a knife !)

Thou enviable being !
No storms, no clouds, in thy blue sky foreseeing,
Play on, play on,
My elfin John !
Toss the light ball—bestride the stick—
(I knew so many cakes would make him sick !)
With fancies, buoyant as the thistle-down,
Prompting the face grotesque, and antic brisk,
With many a lamb-like frisk,
(He's got the scissors, snipping at your gown !)
Thou pretty opening rose !
(Go to your mother, child, and wipe your nose !)
Balmy and breathing music like the south,
(He really brings my heart into my mouth !)
Fresh as the morn, and brilliant as its star,—
(I wish that window had an iron bar !)
Bold as the hawk, yet gentle as the dove,
(I tell you what, my love,
I cannot write unless he's sent above !)

Thomas Hood.

I REMEMBER, I REMEMBER.

I REMEMBER, I remember
The house where I was born,
The little window where the sun
Came peeping in at morn ;
He never came a wink too soon,
Nor brought too long a day,
But now, I often wish the night
Had borne my breath away !

I remember, I remember
The roses, red and white,
The violets, and the lily-cups,
Those flowers made of light !
The lilac where the robin built,
And where my brother set
The laburnum on his birthday—
The tree is living yet !

I remember, I remember
Where I used to swing,
And thought the air must rush as fresh
To swallows on the wing ;
My spirit flew in feathers then,
That is so heavy now,
And summer pools could hardly cool
The fever on my brow !

I remember, I remember
The fir trees dark and high ;
I used to think their slender tops
Were close against the sky :

It was a childish ignorance,
But now 'tis little joy
To know I'm farther off from Heav'n
Than when I was a boy.

Thomas Hood.

A RETROSPECTIVE REVIEW.

OH, when I was a tiny boy,
My days and nights were full of joy,
    My mates were blithe and kind !—
No wonder that I sometimes sigh,
And dash the tear-drop from my eye,
    To cast a look behind !

A hoop was an eternal round
Of pleasure. In those days I found
    A top a joyous thing ;—
But now those past delights I drop,
My head, alas ! is all my top,
    And careful thoughts the string !

My marbles—once my bag was stored,—
Now I must play with Elgin's lord,
    With Theseus for a taw !
My playful horse has slipt his string,
Forgotten all his capering,
    And harness'd to the law !

My kite—how fast and far it flew !
Whilst I, a sort of Franklin, drew
    My pleasure from the sky !

'Twas paper'd o'er with studious themes,
The tasks I wrote—my present dreams
　　Will never soar so high !

My joys are wingless all and dead ;
My dumps are made of more than lead ;
　　My flights soon find a fall ;
My fears prevail, my fancies droop,
Joy never cometh with a hoop,
　　And seldom with a call !

My football's laid upon the shelf ;
I am a shuttlecock myself
　　The world knocks to and fro ;—
My archery is all unlearned,
And grief against myself has turn'd
　　My arrows and my bow !

No more in noontide sun I bask ;
My authorship's an endless task,
　　My head's ne'er out of school :
My heart is pain'd with scorn and slight,
I have too many foes to fight,
　　And friends grown strangely cool !

The very chum that shared my cake
Holds out so cold a hand to shake,
　　It makes me shrink and sigh :—
On this I will not dwell and hang—
The changeling would not feel a pang,
　　Though these should meet his eye !

No skies so blue or so serene
As then ;—no leaves looked half so green
　　As clothed the playground tree !

All things I loved are altered so,
Nor does it ease my heart to know
    That change resides in me !

Oh for the garb that mark'd the boy,
The trousers made of corduroy,
    Well ink'd with black and red ;
The crownless hat, ne'er deem'd an ill—
It only let the sunshine still
    Repose upon my head !

Oh for the riband round the neck !
The careless dogs'-ears apt to check
    My book and collar both !
How can this formal man be styled
Merely an Alexandrine child,
    A boy of larger growth ?

Oh for that small, small beer anew !
And (heaven's own type) that mild sky-blue
    That wash'd my sweet meals down ;
The master even !—and that small Turk
That fagg'd me !—worse is now my work—
    A fag for all the town !

Oh for the lessons learn'd by heart !
Ay, though the very birch's smart
    Should mark these hours again ;
I'd "kiss the rod," and be resign'd
Beneath the stroke, and even find
    Some sugar in the cane !

The Arabian Nights rehearsed in bed !
The Fairy Tales in school-time read,
    By stealth, 'twixt verb and noun !

The angel form that always walk'd
In all my dreams, and look'd, and talk'd
   Exactly like Miss Brown.

The *omne bene*—Christmas come !
The prize of merit, won for home—
   Merit had prizes then !
But now I write for days and days,
For fame—a deal of empty praise,
   Without the silver pen !

Then "home, sweet home !" the crowded coach—
The joyous shout—the loud approach—
   The winding horns like rams' !
The meeting sweet that made me thrill,
The sweetmeats, almost sweeter still,
   No "satis" to the "jams" !—

When that I was a tiny boy
My days and nights were full of joy,
   My mates were blithe and kind !
No wonder that I sometimes sigh,
And dash the tear-drop from my eye,
   To cast a look behind !
                 Thomas Hood.

THE THREE SONS.

I HAVE a son, a little son, a boy just five years old,
With eyes of thoughtful earnestness, and mind of gentle
   mould.
They tell me that unusual grace in all his ways appears,
That my child is grave and wise of heart beyond his
   childish years.

I cannot say how this may be, I know his face is fair,
And yet his chiefest comeliness is his sweet and serious
air.
I know his heart is kind and fond, I know he loveth me,
But loveth yet his mother more with grateful fervency ;
But that which others most admire is the thought which
fills his mind—
The food for grave inquiring speech he everywhere doth
find.
Strange questions doth he ask of me, when we together
walk ;
He scarcely thinks as children think, or talks as children
talk ;
Nor cares he much for childish sports, dotes not on 'bat
or ball,
But looks on manhood's ways and works, and aptly
mimicks all.
His little heart is busy still, and oftentimes perplext
With thoughts about this world of ours, and thoughts
about the next.
He kneels at his dear mother's knee, she teacheth him
to pray,
And strange, and sweet, and solemn then are the words
which he will say.
Oh, should my gentle child be spared to manhood's
years, like me,
A holier and a wiser man I trust that he will be ;
And when I look into his eyes, and stroke his thoughtful
brow,   [now.
I dare not think what I should feel, were I to lose him

I have a son, a second son, a simple child of three ;
I'll not declare how bright and fair his little features be,
How silver sweet those tones of his when he prattles on
my knee.

I do not think his light blue eye is, like his brother's,
    keen,
Nor his brow so full of childish thought as his hath ever
    been;
But his little heart's a fountain pure of kind and tender
    feeling,
And his every look's a gleam of light, rich depths of love
    revealing.
When he walks with me, the country folk who pass us
    in the street
Will shout for joy, and bless my boy, he looks so mild
    and sweet.
A playfellow is he to all, and yet, with cheerful tone,
Will sing his little song of love, when left to sport alone.
His presence is like sunshine sent to gladden home and
    hearth,   [mirth.
To comfort us in all our griefs, and sweeten all our
Should he grow up to riper years, God grant his heart
    may prove
As sweet a home for heavenly grace as now for earthly
    love;   dim,
And if, beside his grave, the tears our aching eyes must
God comfort us for all the love which we shall lose in
    him.

I have a son, a third sweet son, his age I cannot tell,
For they reckon not by years and months where he is
    gone to dwell ;
To us, for fourteen anxious months, his infant smiles
    were given,
And then he bade farewell to earth, and went to live in
    heaven.   [now,
I cannot tell what form his is, what looks he weareth
Nor guess how bright a glory crowns his shining seraph
    brow.

The thoughts that fill his sinless soul, the bliss which he
    doth feel,
Are numbered with the secret things which God will not
    reveal.
But I know (for God hath told me this) that he is now at
    rest,   [breast.
Where other blessed infants be, on their Saviour's loving
I know his spirit feels no more this weary load of flesh,
But his sleep is blessed with endless dreams of joy for
    ever fresh.
I know the angels fold him close beneath their glittering
    wings,
And soothe him with a song that breathes of Heaven's
    divinest things.
I know that we shall meet our babe (his mother dear
    and I)
Where God for aye shall wipe away all tears from every
    eye.
Whate'er befalls his brethren twain, *his* bliss can never
    cease ;
Their lot may here be grief and fear, but *his* is certain
    peace.
It may be that the tempter's wiles their souls from bliss
    may sever,
But, if our own poor faith fail not, *he* must be ours for
    ever.
When we think of what our darling is, and what we still
    must be ;
When we muse on *that* world's perfect bliss, and *this*
    world's misery ;
When we groan beneath this load of sin, and feel this
    grief and pain,
Oh ! we'd rather lose our other two than have him here
    again.

                                        John Moultrie.

SCHOOL AND SCHOOLFELLOWS.

TWELVE years ago I made a mock
    Of filthy trades and traffics,
I wonder'd what they meant by stock ;
    I wrote delightful sapphics :
I knew the streets of Rome and Troy,
    I supp'd with Fates and Furies,—
Twelve years ago I was a boy,
    A happy boy, at Drury's.

Twelve years ago !—how many a thought
    Of faded pains and pleasures
Those whisper'd syllables have brought
    From memory's hoarded treasures !
The fields, the farms, the bats, the books,
    The glories and disgraces,
The voices of dear friends, the looks
    Of old familiar faces !

Kind *Mater* smiles again to me,
    As bright as when we parted ;
I seem again the frank, the free,
    Stout-limb'd, and simple hearted !
Pursuing every idle dream,
    And shunning every warning ;
With no hard work but Bovney stream,
    No chill except Long Morning :

Now stopping Harry Vernon's ball
    That rattled like a rocket ;
Now hearing Wentworth's " Fourteen all ! "
    And striking for the pocket ;

Now feasting on a cheese and flitch,—
 Now drinking from the pewter ;
Now leaping over Chalvey ditch,
 Now laughing at my tutor.

Where are my friends ? I am alone ;
 No playmate shares my beaker ;
Some lie beneath the churchyard stone,
 And some—before the Speaker ;
And some compose a tragedy,
 And some compose a rondo ;
And some draw sword for Liberty,
 And some draw pleas for John Doe.

Tom Mill was used to blacken eyes
 Without the fear of sessions ;
Charles Medlar loathed false quantities,
 As much as false professions ;
Now Mill keeps order in the land,
 A magistrate pedantic ;
And Medlar's feet repose unscann'd
 Beneath the wide Atlantic.

Wild Nick, whose oaths made such a din,
 Does Dr. Martext's duty ;
And Mullion, with that monstrous chin,
 Is married to a Beauty ;
And Darrell studies, week by week,
 His Mant, and not his Manton ;
And Ball, who was but poor at Greek,
 Is very rich at Canton.

And I am eight-and-twenty now ;—
 The world's cold chains have bound me ;
And darker shades are on my brow,
 And sadder scenes around me :

In Parliament I fill my seat,
  With many other noodles ;
And lay my head in Jermyn Street,
  And sip my hock at Boodle's.

But often, when the cares of life
  Have set my temples aching,
When visions haunt me of a wife,
  When duns await my waking,
When Lady Jane is in a pet,
  Or Hoby in a hurry,
When Captain Hazard wins a bet,
  Or Beaulieu spoils a curry,—

For hours and hours I think and talk
  Of each remember'd hobby ;
I long to lounge in Poet's Walk,
  To shiver in the Lobby ;
I wish that I could run away
  From House, and Court, and Leveé,
Where bearded men appear to-day
  Just Eton boys grown heavy,—

That I could bask in childhood's sun
  And dance o'er childhood's roses,
And find huge wealth in one pound one,
  Vast wit in broken noses,
And play Sir Giles at Datchet Lane,
  And call the milkmaids Houris,—
That I could be a boy again,—
  A happy boy,—at Drury's.

Winthrop Mackworth Praed.

SKETCH OF A YOUNG LADY,
FIVE MONTHS OLD.

My pretty, budding, breathing flower,
    Methinks, if I to-morrow
Could manage, just for half-an-hour,
    Sir Joshua's brush to borrow,
I might immortalise a few
    Of all the myriad graces
Which Time, while yet they all are new,
    With newer still replaces.

I'd paint, my child, your deep blue eyes,
    Their quick and earnest flashes ;
I'd paint the fringe that round them lies,
    The fringe of long dark lashes ;
I'd draw with most fastidious care
    One eyebrow, then the other,
And that fair forehead, broad and fair,
    The forehead of your mother.

I'd oft retouch the dimpled cheek
    Where health in sunshine dances ;
And oft the pouting lips, where speak
    A thousand voiceless fancies ;
And the soft neck would keep me long,
    The neck, more smooth and snowy
Than ever yet in schoolboy's song
    Had Caroline or Chloe.

Nor less on those twin rounded arms
    My new-found skill would linger,
Nor less upon the rosy charms
    Of every tiny finger,

Nor slight the small feet, little one,
  So prematurely clever
That, though they neither walk nor run,
  I think they'd jump for ever.

But then your odd endearing ways—
  What study e'er could catch them?
Your aimless gestures, endless plays—
  What canvas e'er could match them?
Your lively leap of merriment,
  Your murmur of petition,
Your serious silence of content,
  Your laugh of recognition.

Here were a puzzling toil, indeed,
  For Art's most fine creations!—
Grow on, sweet baby; we will need
  To note your transformations.
No picture of your form or face,
  Your waking or your sleeping,
But that which Love shall daily trace,
  And trust to Memory's keeping.

Hereafter, when revolving years
  Have made you tall and twenty,
And brought you blended hopes and fears,
  And sighs and slaves in plenty,
May those who watch our little saint
  Among her tasks and duties,
Feel all her virtues hard to paint,
  As now we deem her beauties.

Winthrop Mackworth Praed.

CHILDHOOD AND HIS VISITORS.

ONCE on a time, when sunny May
  Was kissing up the April showers,
I saw fair Childhood hard at play
  Upon a bank of blushing flowers :
Happy—he knew not whence or how,—
  And smiling,—who could choose but love him ?
For not more glad than Childhood's brow,
  Was the blue heaven that beam'd above him.

Old Time, in most appalling wrath,
  That valley's green repose invaded ;
The brooks grew dry upon his path,
  The birds were mute, the lilies faded.
But Time so swiftly wing'd his flight,
  In haste a Grecian tomb to batter,
That Childhood watch'd his paper kite,
  And knew just nothing of the matter.

With curling lip and glancing eye
  Guilt gazed upon the scene a minute ;
But Childhood's glance of purity
  Had such a holy spell within it,
That the dark demon to the air
  Spread forth again his baffled pinion,
And hid his envy and despair,
  Self-tortured, in his own dominion.

Then stepp'd a gloomy phantom up,
  Pale, cypress-crown'd, Night's awful daughter,
And proffer'd him a fearful cup
  Full to the brim of bitter water :

Poor Childhood bade her tell her name ;
    And when the beldame mutter'd—" Sorrow,"
He said,—" Don't interrupt my game ;
    I'll taste it, if I must, to-morrow."

The Muse of Pindus thither came,
    And woo'd him with the softest numbers
That ever scatter'd wealth and fame
    Upon a youthful poet's slumbers ;
Though sweet the music of the lay,
    To Childhood it was all a riddle,
And " Oh," he cried, " do send away
    That noisy woman with the fiddle ! "

Then Wisdom stole his bat and ball,
    And taught him, with most sage endeavour,
Why bubbles rise and acorns fall,
    And why no toy may last for ever.
She talk'd of all the wondrous laws
    Which Nature's open book discloses,
And Childhood, ere she made a pause,
    Was fast asleep among the roses.

Sleep on, sleep on ! oh ! Manhood's dreams
    Are all of earthly pain or pleasure,
Of Glory's toils, Ambition's schemes,
    Of cherish'd love, or hoarded treasure :
But to the couch where Childhood lies
    A more delicious trance is given,
Lit up by rays from seraph eyes,
    And glimpses of remember'd Heaven !

Winthrop Mackworth Praed.

THRENODY.

The south-wind brings
Life, sunshine, and desire,
And on every mount and meadow
Breathes aromatic fire ;
But over the dead he has no power,
The lost, the lost, he cannot restore ;
And, looking over the hills, I mourn
The darling who shall not return.

I see my empty house,
I see my trees repair their boughs ;
And he, the wondrous child,
Whose silver warble wild
Outvalued every pulsing sound
Within the air's cerulean round—
The hyacinthine boy, for whom
Morn well might break and April bloom—
The gracious boy, who did adorn
The world whereinto he was born,
And by his countenance repay
The favour of the loving Day—
Has disappeared from the Day's eye ;
Far and wide she cannot find him ;
My hopes pursue, they cannot bind him.

Returned this day, the south-wind searches,
And finds young pines and budding birches ;
But finds not the budding man ;
Nature who lost, cannot remake him ;
Fate let him fall, Fate cannot retake him ;
Nature, Fate, men, him seek in vain.

And whither now, my truant wise and sweet,
O, whither tend thy feet ?

I had the right, few days ago,
Thy steps to watch, thy place to know ;
How have I forfeited the right?
Hast thou forgot me in a new delight ?
I hearken for thy household cheer,
O eloquent child !
Whose voice, an equal messenger,
Conveyed thy meaning mild.
What though the pains and joys
Whereof it spoke were toys
Fitting his age and ken,
Yet fairest dames and bearded men,
Who heard the sweet request,
So gentle, wise, and grave,
Bended with joy to his behest,
And let the world's affairs go by,
A while to share his cordial game,
Or mend his wicker waggon-frame,
Still plotting how their hungry ear
That winsome voice again might hear ;
For his lips could well pronounce
Words that were persuasions.

Gentlest guardians marked serene
His early hope, his liberal mien ;
Took counsel from his guiding eyes
To make this wisdom earthly wise.
Ah, vainly do these eyes recall
The school-march, each day's festival,
When every morn my bosom glowed
To watch the convoy on the road ;
The babe in willow waggon closed,
With rolling eyes and face composed ;
With children forward and behind,
Like Cupids studiously inclined ;

And he the chieftain paced beside,
The centre of the troop allied,
With sunny face of sweet repose,
To guard the babe from fancied foes.
The little captain innocent
Took the eye with him as he went ;
Each village senior paused to scan
And speak the lovely caravan.
From the window I look out
To mark thy beautiful parade,
Stately marching in cap and coat
To some tune by fairies played—
A music heard by thee alone
To works as noble led thee on.
Now Love and Pride, alas ! in vain,
Up and down their glances strain.
The painted sled stands where it stood ;
The kennel by the corded wood ;
His gathered sticks to staunch the wall
Of the snow-tower, when snow should fall ;
The ominous hole he dug in the sand,
And childhood's castles built or planned ;
His daily haunts I well discern—
The poultry-yard, the shed, the barn—
And every inch of garden ground
Paced by the blessed feet around,
From the roadside to the brook
Whereinto he loved to look.
Step the meek birds where erst they ranged ;
The wintry garden lies unchanged ;
The brook into the stream runs on ;
But the deep-eyed boy is gone.

On that shaded day,
Dark with more clouds than tempests are,

When thou didst yield thy innocent breath
In bird-like heavings unto death,
Night came, and Nature had not thee;
I said, "We are mates in misery."
The morrow dawned with needless glow :
Each snowbird chirped, each fowl must crow ;
Each tramper started, but the feet
Of the most beautiful and sweet
Of human youth had left the hill
And garden—they were bound and still.
There's not a sparrow or a wren,
There's not a blade of autumn grain,
Which the four seasons do not tend,
And tides of life and increase end ;
And every chick of every bird,
And weed and rock-moss is preferred.

O ostrich-like forgetfulness !
O loss of larger in the less !
Was there no star that could be sent,
No watcher in the firmament,
No angel from the countless host
That loiters round the crystal coast,
Could stoop to heal that only child,
Nature's sweet marvel undefiled,
And keep the blossom of the earth,
Which all her harvests were not worth ?
Not mine—I never called thee mine,
But Nature's heir—if I repine,
And seeing rashly torn and moved
Not what I made, but what I loved,
Grow early old with grief that thou
Must to the wastes of Nature go—
'Tis because a general hope
Was quenched, and all must doubt and grope.

For flattering planets seemed to say
This child should ills of ages stay,
By wondrous tongue, and guided pen,
Bring the flown Muses back to men.
Perchance not he but Nature ailed ;
The world, and not the infant failed.
It was not ripe yet to sustain
A genius of so fine a strain,
Who gazed upon the sun and moon
As if he came unto his own,
And, pregnant with his grander thought,
Brought the old order into doubt.
His beauty once their beauty tried ;
They could not feed him, and he died,
And wandered backward as in scorn,
To wait an æon to be born.
Ill day which made this beauty waste,
Plight broken, this high face defaced !
Some went and came about the dead ;
And some in books of solace read ;
Some to their friends the tidings say ;
Some went to write, some went to pray ;
One tarried here, there hurried one ;
But their heart abode with none.
Covetous death bereaved us all,
To aggrandise one funeral.
The eager fate which carried thee
Took the largest part of me ;
For this losing is true dying ;
This is lordly man's down-lying,
This is slow but sure reclining,
Star by star his world resigning.
O child of paradise !
Boy who made dear his father's home,
In whose deep eyes

Men read the welfare of the times to come,
I am too much bereft.
The world dishonoured thou hast left.
O truth's and Nature's costly lie !
O trusted broken prophecy !
O richest fortune sourly crossed !
Born for the future, to the future lost !

The deep Heart answered, "Weepest thou ?
Worthier cause for passion wild
If I had not taken the child.
And deemest thou as those who pore,
With aged eyes, short way before—
Think'st Beauty vanished from the coast
Of Matter, and thy darling lost ?
Taught he not thee—the Man of eld,
Whose eyes within his eyes beheld
Heaven's numerous hierarchy span
The mystic gulf from God to man ?
To be alone wilt thou begin
When worlds of lovers hem thee in ?
To-morrow when the masks shall fall
That dizen Nature's carnival,
The pure shall see by their own will,
Which overflowing Love shall fill,
'Tis not within the force of fate
The fate-conjoined to separate.
But thou, my votary, weepest thou ?
I gave thee sight—where is it now ?
I taught thy heart beyond the reach
Of ritual, bible, or of speech ;
Wrote in thy mind's transparent table,
As far as the communicable ;
Taught thee each private sign to raise,
Lit by the supersolar blaze.

Past utterance, and past belief,
And past the blasphemy of grief,
The mysteries of Nature's art ;
And though no Muse can these impart,
Throb thine with Nature's throbbing breast,
And all is clear from east to west.

" I came to thee as to a friend ;
Dearest, to thee I did not send
Tutors, but a joyful eye,
Innocence that matched the sky,
Lovely locks, a form of wonder,
Laughter rich as woodland thunder,
That thou might'st entertain apart
The richest flowering of all art :
And, as the great all-loving Day
Through smallest chambers takes its way,
That thou might'st break thy daily bread
With prophet, Saviour, and head ;
That thou might'st cherish for thine own
The riches of sweet Mary's Son,
Boy-Rabbi, Israel's paragon.
And thoughtest thou such guest
Would in thy hall take up his rest ?
Would rushing life forget her laws,
Fate's glowing revolution pause ?
High omens ask diviner guess ;
Not to be conned to tediousness.
And know my higher gifts unbind
The zone that girds the incarnate mind.
When the scanty shores are full
With Thought's perilous, whirling pool ;
When frail Nature can no more,
Then the Spirit strikes the hour :

My servant Death, with solving rite,
Pours finite into infinite.

" Wilt thou freeze love's tidal flow,
Whose streams through Nature circling go?
Nail the wild star to its track
On the half-climbed zodiac?
Light is light which radiates,
Blood is blood which circulates,
Life is life which generates,
And many-seeming life is one—
Wilt thou transfix and make it none?
Its onward force too starkly pent
In figure, bone, and lineament?
Wilt thou, uncalled, interrogate,
Talker! the unreplying Fate?
Nor see the genius of the whole
Ascendant in the private soul,
Beckon it when to go and come,
Self-announced its hour of doom?
Fair the soul's recess and shrine,
Magic-built to last a season ;
Masterpiece of love benign ;
Fairer that expansive reason,
Whose omen 'tis and sign.
Wilt thou not ope thy heart to know
What rainbows teach, and sunsets show?
Verdict which accumulates
From lengthening scroll of human fates,
Voice of earth to earth returned,
Prayers of saints that inly burned—
Saying, *What is excellent,*
As God lives, is permanent ;
Hearts are dust, hearts' loves remain ;
Heart's love will meet thee again

Revere the Maker; fetch thine eye
Up to his style, and manners of the sky.
Not of adamant and gold
Built He heaven stark and cold;
No, but a nest of bending reeds,
Flowering grass, and scented weeds;
Or like a traveller's fleeing tent,
Or bow above the tempest bent;
Built of tears and sacred flames,
And virtue reaching to its aims;
Built of furtherance and pursuing,
Not of spent deeds, but of doing.
Silent rushes the swift Lord
Through ruined systems still restored,
Broad-sowing, bleak and void to bless,
Plants with worlds the wilderness;
Waters with tears of ancient sorrow
Apples of Eden ripe to-morrow.
House and tenant go to ground,
Lost in God, in Godhead found."

Ralph Waldo Emerson.

THE REAPER AND THE FLOWERS.

THERE is a Reaper, whose name is Death,
  And, with his sickle keen,
He reaps the bearded grain at a breath,
  And the flowers that grow between.

"Shall I have nought that is fair," saith he;
  "Have nought but the bearded grain?
Though the breath of these flowers is sweet to me,
  I will give them all back again."

He gazed at the flowers with tearful eyes,
  He kissed their drooping leaves ;
It was for the Lord of Paradise
  He bound them in his sheaves.

" My Lord has need of these flowerets gay,"
  The Reaper said, and smiled ;
" Dear tokens of the earth are they,
  Where He was once a child.

" They shall all bloom in fields of light,
  Transplanted by my care,
And saints, upon their garments white,
  These sacred blossoms wear."

And the mother gave, in tears and pain,
  The flowers she most did love ;
She knew she should find them all again
  In the fields of light above.

Oh, not in cruelty, not in wrath,
  The Reaper came that day ;
Twas an angel visited the green earth,
  And took the flowers away.

                    Henry Wadsworth Longfellow.

CHILDREN.

COME to me, O ye children !
  For I hear you at your play,
And the questions that perplexed me
  Have vanished quite away.

Ye open the eastern windows,
    That look towards the sun,
Where thoughts are singing swallows,
    And the brooks of morning run.

In your hearts are the birds and the sunshine,
    In your thoughts the brooklet's flow,
But in mine is the wind of Autumn,
    And the first fall of the snow.

Ah ! what would the world be to us,
    If the children were no more?
We should dread the desert behind us
    Worse than the dark before.

What the leaves are to the forest,
    With light and air for food,
Ere their sweet and tender juices
    Have been hardened into wood,—

That to the world are children ;
    Through them it feels the glow
Of a brighter and sunnier climate
    Than reaches the trunks below.

Come to me, O ye children !
    And whisper in my ear
What the birds and the winds are singing
    In your sunny atmosphere.

For what are all our contrivings,
    And the wisdom of our books,
When compared with your caresses,
    And the gladness of your looks.

Ye are better than all the ballads
  That ever were sung or said ;
For ye are living poems,
  And all the rest are dead.

                    Henry Wadsworth Longfellow.

THE CHILDREN'S HOUR.

BETWEEN the dark and the daylight,
  When the night is beginning to lower,
Comes a pause in the day's occupation,
  That is known as the Children's Hour.

I hear in the chamber above me
  The patter of little feet,
The sound of a door that is opened,
  And voices soft and sweet.

From my study I see in the lamplight,
  Descending the broad hall stair,
Grave Alice and laughing Allegra,
  And Edith with golden hair.

A whisper and then a silence ;
  Yet I know by their merry eyes
They are plotting and planning together
  To take me by surprise.

A sudden rush from the stairway,
  A sudden raid from the hall !
By three doors left unguarded
  They enter my castle wall !

They climb up into my turret
   O'er the arms and back of my chair ;
If I try to escape they surround me ;
   They seem to be everywhere.

They almost devour me with kisses,
   Their arms about me entwine,
Till I think of the Bishop of Bingen
   In his Mouse Tower on the Rhine !

Do you think, O blue-eyed banditti,
   Because you have scaled the wall,
Such an old moustache as I am
   Is not a match for you all !

I have you fast in my fortress,
   And will not let you depart,
But put you down into the dungeon
   In the round-tower of my heart.

And there will I keep you for ever,
   Yes, for ever and a day,
Till the walls shall crumble to ruin,
   And moulder in dust away !

          Henry Wadsworth Longfellow.

THE WRECK OF THE HESPERUS.

IT was the schooner Hesperus,
   That sailed the wintry sea ;
And the skipper had taken his little daughter,
   To bear him company.

Blue were her eyes as the fairy-flax,
　　Her cheeks like the dawn of day,
And her bosom white as the hawthorn buds,
　　That ope in the month of May.

The skipper he stood beside the helm,
　　His pipe was in his mouth,
And he watched how the veering flaw did blow
　　The smoke now West, now South.

Then up and spake an old Sailòr,
　　Had sailed the Spanish Main,
"I pray thee, put into yonder port,
　　For I fear a hurricane.

"Last night the moon had a golden ring,
　　And to-night no moon we see !"
The skipper he blew a whiff from his pipe,
　　And a scornful laugh laughed he.

Colder and louder blew the wind,
　　A gale from the North-east ;
The snow fell hissing in the brine,
　　And the billows frothed like yeast.

Down came the storm, and smote amain
　　The vessel in its strength ;
She shuddered and paused, like a frighted steed,
　　Then leaped her cable's length.

"Come hither ! come hither ! my little daughtèr,
　　And do not tremble so ;
For I can weather the roughest gale
　　That ever wind did blow."

He wrapped her warm in his seaman's coat,
 Against the stinging blast;
He cut a rope from a broken spar,
 And bound her to the mast.

" O father ! I hear the church-bells ring,
 O say what may it be?"
" 'Tis a fog-bell on a rock-bound coast !"—
 And he steered for the open sea.

" O father ! I hear the sound of guns,
 O say, what may it be?"
" Some ship in distress, that cannot live
 In such an angry sea !"

" O father ! I see a gleaming light,
 O say, what may it be?"
But the father answered never a word,
 A frozen corpse was he.

Lashed to the helm, all stiff and stark,
 With his face turned to the skies,
The lantern gleamed through the gleaming snow
 On his fixed and glassy eyes.

Then the maiden clasped her hands and prayed,
 That savèd she might be ;
And she thought of Christ, who stilled the wave,
 On the Lake of Galilee.

And fast through the midnight dark and drear,
 Through the whistling sleet and snow,
Like a sheeted ghost the vessel swept
 Tow'rds the reef of Norman's Woe.

And ever the fitful gusts between,
  A sound came from the land;
It was the sound of the trampling surf,
  On the rocks and the hard sea-sand.

The breakers were right beneath her bows,
  She drifted a dreary wreck,
And a whooping billow swept the crew
  Like icicles from her deck.

She struck where the white and fleecy waves
  Looked soft as carded wool,
But the cruel rocks, they gored her side
  Like the horns of an angry bull.

Her rattling shrouds, all sheathed in ice,
  With the masts went by the board;
Like a vessel of glass, she stove and sank,
  Ho! ho! the breakers roared!

At daybreak, on the black sea-beach,
  A fisherman stood aghast,
To see the form of a maiden fair,
  Lashed close to a drifting mast.

The salt sea was frozen on her breast,
  The salt tears in her eyes;
And he saw her hair, like the brown sea-weed,
  On the billows fall and rise.

Such was the wreck of the Hesperus,
  In the midnight and the snow;
Christ save us all from a death like this,
  On the reef of Norman's Woe!

            Henry Wadsworth Longfellow.

THE BAREFOOT BOY.

BLESSINGS on thee, little man,
Barefoot boy, with cheeks of tan !
With thy turned-up pantaloons
And thy merry whistled tunes;
With thy red lip, redder still
Kissed by strawberries on the hill ;
With the sunshine on thy face
Through thy torn brim's jaunty grace ;
From my heart I give thee joy,—
I was once a barefoot boy !
Prince thou art—the grown-up man
Only is Republican.
Let the million-dollared ride !
Barefoot, trudging at his side,
Thou hast more than he can buy
In the reach of ear and eye—
Outward sunshine, inward joy,
Blessings on the barefoot boy !

O for boyhood's painless play,
Sleep that wakes in laughing day,
Health that mocks the doctor's rules,
Knowledge never learned of schools,
Of the wild bee's morning chase,
Of the wild flowers' time and place,
Flight of fowl and habitude
Of the tenants of the wood ;
How the tortoise bears his shell ;
How the woodchuck digs his cell,
And the ground mole sinks his well ;
How the robin feeds her young,
How the oriole's nest is hung ;

Where the whitest lilies blow,
Where the freshest berries grow,
Where the ground nut trails its vine,
Where the wood grape's clusters shine :
Of the black wasp's cunning way,
Mason of his walls of clay,
And the architectural plans
Of grey hornet artisans !—
For, eschewing books and tasks,
Nature answers all he asks ;
Hand in hand with her he walks,
Face to face with her he talks,
Part and parcel of her joy—
Blessings on the barefoot boy !

O for boyhood's time of June,
Crowding years in one brief moon,
When all things I heard or saw,
Me, their master, waited for.
I was rich in flowers and trees,
Humming-birds and honey-bees ;
For my sport the squirrel played,
Plied the snouted mole his spade ;
For my taste the blackberry cone
Purpled over hedge and stone ;
Laughed the brook for my delight
Through the day and through the night ;
Whispering at the garden wall,
Talked with me from fall to fall ;
Mine the sand-rimmed pickeril pond,
Mine the walnut slopes beyond,
Mine, on bending orchard trees,
Apples of Hesperides !
Still as my horizon grew,

Larger grew my riches too,
All the world I saw or knew
Seemed a complex Chinese toy,
Fashioned for a barefoot boy !

O for festal dainties spread,
Like my bowl of milk and bread—
Pewter spoon and bowl of wood,
On the door stone, grey and rude !
O'er me, like a regal tent,
Cloudy-ribbed, the sunset bent,
Purple-curtained, fringed with gold,
Looped in many a wide-swung fold ;
While for music came the play
Of the pied frogs' orchestra ;
And, to light the noisy choir,
Lit the fly his lamp of fire.
I was monarch : pomp and joy
Waited on the barefoot boy !

Cheerily, then, my little man,
Live and laugh, as boyhood can !
Though the flinty slopes be hard,
Stubble-speared the new-mown sward,
Every morn shall lead thee through
Fresh baptisms of the dew ;
Every evening from thy feet
Shall the cool wind kiss the heat,
All too soon these feet must hide
In the prison cells of pride,
Lose the freedom of the sod,
Like a colt's for work be shod,
Made to tread the mills of toil,
Up and down in ceaseless moil ;

Happy if their track be found
Never on forbidden ground ;
Happy if they sink not in
Quick and treacherous sands of sin.
Ah ! that thou couldst know thy joy,
Ere it passes, barefoot boy !

John Greenleaf Whittier.

VESTA.

O CHRIST of God ! whose life and death
  Our own have reconciled,
Most quietly, most tenderly
  Take home thy star-named child !

Thy grace is in her patient eyes,
  Thy words are on her tongue ;
The very silence round her seems
  As if the angels sung.

Her smile is as a listening child's
  Who hears its mother call ;
The lilies of Thy perfect peace
  About her pillow fall.

She leans from out our clinging arms
  To rest herself in Thine ;
Alone to Thee, dear Lord, can we
  Our well-beloved resign !

O, less for her than for ourselves
  We bow our heads and pray ;
Her setting star, like Bethlehem's,
  To Thee shall point the way !

John Greenleaf Whittier.

IN SCHOOL-DAYS.

STILL sits the school-house by the road,
  A ragged beggar sunning ;
Around it still the sumachs grow,
  And blackberry vines are running.

Within the master's desk is seen,
  Deep scarred by raps official ;
The warping floor, the battered seats,
  The jack-knife's carved initial ;

The charcoal frescoes on its wall ;
  Its door's worn sill, betraying
The feet that, creeping slow to school,
  Went storming out to playing !

Long years ago a winter sun
  Shone over it at setting ;
Lit up its western window-panes,
  And low eaves' icy fretting.

It touched the tangled golden curls,
  And brown eyes full of grieving,
Of one who still her steps delayed
  When all the school were leaving.

For near her stood the little boy
  Her childish favour singled ;
His cap pulled low upon a face
  Where pride and shame were mingled.

Pushing with restless feet the snow
  To right and left, he lingered ;—
As restlessly her tiny hands
  The blue-checked apron fingered.

He saw her lift her eyes ; he felt
The soft hand's light caressing,
And heard the tremble of her voice,
As if a fault confessing.

" I'm sorry that I spelt the word :
I hate to go above you,
Because,"—the brown eyes lower fell,—
" Because, you see, I love you ! "

Still memory to a grey-haired man
That sweet child-face is showing.
Dear girl ! the grasses on her grave
Have forty years been growing !

He lives to learn in life's hard school,
How few who pass above him
Lament their triumph and his loss,
Like her,—because they love him.

John Greenleaf Whittier.

CHILD-SONGS.

STILL linger in our noon of time
And our Saxon tongue
The echoes of the home-born hymns
The Aryan mothers sung.

And childhood had its litanies
In every age and clime ;
The earliest cradles of the race
Were rocked to poet's rhyme.

Nor sky, nor wave, nor tree, nor flower,
Nor green earth's virgin sod,
So moved the singer's heart of old
As these small ones of God.

The mystery of unfolding life
Was more than dawning morn,
Than opening flower or crescent moon—
The human soul new-born !

And still to childhood's sweet appeal
The heart of genius turns,
And more than all the sages teach
From lisping voices learns,—

The voices loved of him who sang,
Where Tweed and Teviot glide,
That sound to-day on all the winds
That blow from Rydal side,—

Heard in the Teuton's household songs,
And folk-lore of the Finn,
Where'er to holy Christmas hearths
The Christ-child enters in !

Before life's sweetest mystery still
The heart in reverence kneels ;
The wonder of the primal birth
The latest mother feels.

We need love's tender lessons taught
As only weakness can ;
God hath his small interpreters ;
The child must teach the man.

We wander wide through evil years,
Our eyes of faith grow dim ;
But he is freshest from his hands
And nearest unto Him !

And haply, pleading long with Him
For sin-sick hearts and cold,
The angels of our childhood still
The Father's face behold.

Of such the kingdom !—Teach thou us,
O Master most divine,
To feel the deep significance
Of these wise words of thine !

The haughty eye shall seek in vain
What innocence beholds ;
No cunning finds the keys of heaven,
No strength its gate unfolds.

Alone to guilelessness and love
That gate shall open fall ;
The mind of pride is nothingness,
The childlike heart is all !

John Greenleaf Whittier.

RED RIDING-HOOD.

On the wide lawn the snow lay deep
Ridged o'er with many a drifted heap ;
The wind that through the pine-trees sung,
The naked elm-boughs tossed and swung ;
While, through the window, frosty-starred
Against the sunset-purple barred,

We saw the sombre crow flap by,
The hawk's grey fleck along the sky,
The crested blue-jay flitting swift,
The squirrel poising on the drift,
Erect, alert, his broad grey tail
Set to the north wind like a sail.

It came to pass, one little lass,
With flattened face against the glass,
And eyes in which the tender dew
Of pity shone, stood gazing through
The narrow space her rosy lips
Had melted from the frost's eclipse;
" O, see," she cried, " the poor blue-jays !
What is it that the black crow says ?
The squirrel lifts his little legs
Because he has no hands, and begs ;
He's asking for my nuts, I know :
May I not feed them on the snow ? "

Half lost within her boots, her head
Warm-sheltered in her hood of red,
Her plaid skirt close about her drawn,
She floundered down the wintry lawn ;
Now struggling through the misty veil
Blown round her by the shrieking gale ;
Now sinking in a drift so low,
Her scarlet hood could scarcely show
Its dash of colour on the snow.

She dropped for bird and beast forlorn
Her little store of nuts and corn,
And thus her timid guests bespoke :—
" Come, squirrel, from your hollow oak—

Come, black old crow—come poor blue-jay,
Before your supper's blown away !
Don't be afraid, we all are good ;
And I'm mamma's Red Riding-Hood ! "

O Thou whose care is over all,
Who heedest even the sparrow's fall,
Keep in the little maiden's breast
The pity which is now its guest !
Let not her cultured years make less
The childhood charm of tenderness,
But let her feel as well as know,
Nor harder with her polish grow !
Unmoved by sentimental grief
That wails along some printed leaf,
But prompt with kindly word and deed
To own the claims of all who need ;
Let the grown woman's self make good
The promise of Red Riding-Hood !

John Greenleaf Whittier.

CREEP AFORE YE GANG.

CREEP awa', my bairnie, creep afore ye gang,
Cock ye baith your lugs to your auld Granny's sang ;
Gin ye gang as far ye will think the road lang—
Creep awa', my bairnie, creep afore ye gang.

Creep awa', my bairnie, ye're ower young to learn
To tot up and down yet, my bonnie wee bairn ;
Better creeping cannie, than fa'ing wi' a bang,
Duntin' a' your wee brow—creep afore ye gang.

Ye'll creep, an' ye'll laugh, an' ye'll nod to your mother,
Watching ilka step o' your wee dowsy brother;
Rest ye on the floor till your wee limbs grow strang,
And ye'll be a braw chield yet—creep afore ye gang.

The wee birdie fa's when it tries ower soon to flee;
Folks are sure to tumble when they climb ower hie;
They wha dinna walk aright are sure to come to
    wrang—
Creep awa', my bairnie, creep afore ye gang.

James Ballantine.

MY CHILD.

My child, we were two children,
Small, merry by childhood's law;
We used to crawl to the hen-house,
And hide ourselves in the straw.

We crowed like cocks, and whenever
The pursuers near us drew—
Cock-a-doodle! they thought
'Twas a real cock that crew.

The boxes about our courtyard
We carpeted to our mind,
And lived there both together—
Kept house in a noble kind.

The neighbour's old cat often
Came to pay us a visit;
We made her a bow and curtscy,
Each with a compliment in it.

After her health we asked,
Our care and regard to evince—
(We have made the very same speeches
To many an old cat since).

We also sate and wisely
Discoursed, as old folks do,
Complaining how all went better
In those good times we knew—

How love, and truth, and believing,
Had left the world to itself,
And how so dear was the coffee,
And how so scarce was the pelf.

The children's games are over,
The rest is over with youth—
The world, the good games, the good times,
The belief, and the love, and the truth.

Elizabeth Barrett Browning.

THE CRY OF THE CHILDREN.

Do ye hear the children weeping, O my brothers,
Ere the sorrow comes with years?
They are leaning their young heads against their
mothers,
And *that* cannot stop their tears.
The young lambs are bleating in the meadows,
The young birds are chirping in the nest,
The young fawns are playing with the shadows,
The young flowers are blowing toward the west—

But the young, young children, O my brothers,
They are weeping bitterly !
They are weeping in the playtime of the others,
In the country of the free.

Do you question the young children in the sorrow,
Why their tears are falling so ?
The old man may weep for his to-morrow
Which is lost in Long ago.
The old tree is leafless in the forest,
The old year is ending in the frost,
The old wound, if stricken, is the sorest,
The old hope is hardest to be lost.
But the young, young children, O my brothers,
Do you ask them why they stand
Weeping sore before the bosoms of their mothers,
In our happy Fatherland ?

They look up with their pale and sunken faces,
And their looks are sad to see,
For the man's hoary anguish draws and presses
Down the cheeks of infancy.
" Your old earth," they say, " is very dreary;
Our young feet," they say, " are very weak !
Few paces have we taken, yet are weary—
Our grave-rest is very far to seek.
Ask the aged why they weep, and not the children ;
For the outside earth is cold ;
And we young ones stand without, in our bewildering,
And the graves are for the old."

" True," say the children, " it may happen
That we die before our time.
Little Alice died last year—her grave is shapen
Like a snowball, in the rime.

We looked into the pit prepared to take her.
Was no room for any work in the close clay !
From the sleep wherein she lieth none will wake her,
Crying, ' Get up, little Alice, it is day."
If you listen by that grave, in sun and shower,
With your ear down, little Alice never cries.
Could we see her face, be sure we should not know her,
For the smile has time for growing in her eyes.
And merry go her moments, lulled and stilled in
The shroud by the kirk-chime !
" It is good when it happens," say the children,
" That we die before our time."

Alas, alas, the children ! they are seeking
Death in life, as best to have.
They are binding up their hearts away from breaking,
With a cerement from a grave.
Go out, children, from the mine and from the city,
Sing out, children, as the little thrushes do.
Pluck your handfuls of the meadow-cowslips pretty,
Laugh aloud, to feel your fingers let them through !
But they answer, are your cowslips of the meadows
Like our weeds a-near the mine ?
Leave us quiet in the dark of the coal-shadows,
From your pleasures fair and fine !

" For oh," say the children, " we are weary
And we cannot run or leap.
If we cared for any meadows, it were merely
To drop down in them and sleep.
Our knees tremble sorely in the stooping,
We fall upon our faces, trying to go ;
And, underneath our heavy eyelids drooping,
The reddest flower would look as pale as snow.
For, all day, we drag our burdens tiring

Through the coal-dark, underground—
Or all day we drive the wheels of iron
In the factories, round and round.

" For, all day, the wheels are droning, turning—
Their wind comes in our faces—
Till our hearts turn—our head, with pulses burning,
And the walls turn in their places.
Turns the sky in the high window blank and reeling,
Turns the long light that drops adown the wall,
Turn the black flies that crawl along the ceiling,
All are turning, all the day, and we with all.
And all day the iron wheels are droning,
And sometimes we could pray,
' O ye wheels ' (breaking out in mad moaning),
' Stop ! be silent for to-day ! ' "

Ay ! be silent !   Let them hear each other breathing
For a moment, mouth to mouth !
Let them touch each other's hands, in a fresh
        wreathing
Of their tender human youth !
Let them feel that this cold metallic motion
Is nor all the life God fashions or reveals.
Let them prove their living souls against the notion
That they live in you, or under you, O wheels !—
Still, all day, the iron wheels go onward,
Grinding life down from its mark ;
And the children's souls, which God is calling sunward,
Spin on blindly in the dark.

Now tell the poor young children, O my brothers,
To look up to Him and pray ;
So the blessed One who blesseth all the others,
Will bless them another day.

They answer, " Who is God that He should hear us,
While the rushing of the iron wheel is stirred ?
When we sob aloud, the human creatures near us,
Pass by, hearing not, or answer not a word.
And *we* hear not (for the wheels in their resounding)
Strangers speaking at the door.
Is it likely God, with angels singing round him,
Hears our weeping any more?

" Two words, indeed, of praying we remember,
And at midnight's hour of harm,
' Our Father,' looking upward in the chamber,
We say softly for a charm.
We know no other words, except ' Our Father,'
And we think that, in some pause of angels' song,
God may pluck them with the silence sweet to gather,
And hold both within his right hand which is strong.
' Our Father ! ' If He heard us, He would surely
(For they call Him good and mild)
Answer, smiling down the steep world very purely,
' Come and rest with me, my child.'

" But no ! " say the children, weeping faster,
" He is speechless as a stone.
And they tell us of His image is the master
Who commands us to work on.
Go to ! " say the children—" up in Heaven,
Dark, wheel-like, turning clouds are all we find.
Do not mock us ; grief has made us unbelieving—
We look up for God, but tears have made us blind."
Do you hear the children weeping and disproving,
O my brothers, what ye preach ?
For God's possible is taught by His world's loving,
And the children doubt of each.

And well may the children weep before you !
They are weary ere they run.
They have never seen the sunshine, nor the glory,
Which is brighter than the sun.
They know the grief of man, without his wisdom;
They sink in man's despair, without its calm ;
Are slaves, without the liberty in Christdom,
Are martyrs, by the pang without the palm—
Are worn, as if with age, yet unretrievingly
The harvest of its memories cannot reap—
Are orphans of the earthly love and heavenly.
Let them weep ! let them weep !

They look up, with their pale and sunken faces,
And their look is dread to see,
For they mind you of their angels in high places,
With eyes turned on Deity !
" How long," they say, " how long, O cruel nation,
Will you stand, to move the world, on a child's heart —
Stifle down with a mailed heel its palpitation,
And tread onward to your throne amid the mart ?
Our blood splashes upward, O gold-heaper,
And your purple shows your path !
But the child's sob in the silence curses deeper
Than the strong man in his wrath."

Elizabeth Barrett Browning.

A PORTRAIT.

I WILL paint her as I see her ;
  Ten times have the lilies blown
  Since she looked upon the sun.

And her face is lily-clear,
  Lily-shaped, and dropped in duty
  To the law of its own beauty.

Oval cheeks encoloured faintly,
  Which a taint of golden hair
  Keeps from fading off to air.

And a forehead fair and saintly,
  Which two blue eyes undershine,
  Like meek prayers before a shrine.

Face and figure of a child,—
  Though too calm, you think, and tender,
  For the childhood you would lend her.

Yet child—simple, undefiled,
  Frank, obedient,—waiting still
  On the turning of your will.

Throwing light, as all your things,
  As young birds, or early wheat,
  When the wind blows over it.

Only, free from flutterings
  Of loud mirth that scorneth measure—
  Taking love for her chief pleasure.

Choosing pleasures, for the rest,
  Which come softly—just as she
  When she settles at your knee.

Quiet talk she liketh best,
  In a bower of gentle looks—
  Watering flowers, or reading books.

And her voice, it murmurs lowly
  As a silver stream may run,
  Which yet feels, you feel, the sun.

And her smile it seems half holy,
  As if drawn from thoughts more fair
  Then our common jestings are.

And if any poet knew her
  He would sing of her with falls
  Used in loving madrigals.

And if any painter drew her
  He would paint her unaware
  With a halo round the hair.

And if reader read the poem,
  He would whisper, "You have done a
  Consecrated little Una."

And a dreamer (did you show him
  That same picture) would exclaim,
  "'Tis my angel with a name!"

And a stranger when he sees her
  In the street even—smileth stilly
  Just as you would at a lily.

And all voices that address her
  Soften, sleeker every word,
  As if speaking to a bird.

And all fancies yearn to cover
  The hard earth whereon she passes,
  With the thymy scented grasses.

And all hearts do pray "God love her !"—
  Ay, and always in good sooth,
  We may all be sure HE DOTH.

                    Elizabeth Barrett Browning.

LETTY'S GLOBE.

WHEN Letty had scarce passed her third glad year,
And her young, artless words began to flow,
One day we gave the child a coloured sphere
Of the wide earth, that she might mark and know,
By tint and outline, all its sea and land.
She patted all the world; old empires peep'd
Between her baby-fingers; her soft hand
Was welcome at all frontiers.   How she leaped
And laughed and prattled in her world-wide bliss !
But when we turned her sweet unlearned eye
On our own isle, she raised a joyous cry—
"Oh, yes ! I see it : Letty's home is there !"
And while she hid all England with a kiss,
Bright over Europe fell her golden hair.

                    Charles Tennyson-Turner.

AS THROUGH THE LAND.

As thro' the land at eve we went,
  And pluck'd the ripen'd ears,
We fell out, my wife and I,
O we fell out I know not why,
  And kiss'd again with tears.
And blessings on the falling out
  That all the more endears,
When we fall out with those we love
  And kiss again with tears !
For when we came where lies the child
  We lost in other years,
There above his little grave,
O there above his little grave,
  We kiss'd again with tears.

Lord Tennyson.

SWEET AND LOW.

Sweet and low, sweet and low,
  Wind of the western sea,
Low, low, breathe and blow,
  Wind of the western sea !
Over the rolling waters go,
Come from the dying moon and blow,
  Blow him again to me ;
While my little one, while my pretty one, sleeps.

Sleep and rest, sleep and rest,
  Father will come to thee soon ;
Rest, rest on mother's breast,
  Father will come to thee soon ;

Father will come to his babe in the nest,
Silver sails all out of the west
  Under the silver moon:
Sleep, my little one, sleep, my pretty one, sleep.

Lord Tennyson.

IN THE CHILDREN'S HOSPITAL.

EMMIE.

I.

OUR doctor had call'd in another, I never had seen him
  before,
But he sent a chill to my heart when I saw him come in
  at the door,
Fresh from the surgery-schools of France and of other
  lands—
Harsh red hair, big voice, big chest, big merciless hands!
Wonderful cures he had done, O yes; but they said too
  of him
He was happier using the knife than in trying to save
  the limb,   [so red,
And that I can well believe, for he look'd so coarse and
I could think he was one of those who would break their
  jests on the dead,
And mangle the living dog that had loved him and
  fawn'd at his knee—
Drench'd with the hellish oorali—that even such things
  should be!

II.

Here was a boy—I am sure that some of our children
  would die
But for the voice of Love, and the smile, and the com-
  forting eye—

Here was a boy in the ward, every bone seem'd out of
    its place—
Caught in a mill and crush'd—it was all but a hopeless
    case :
And he handled him quietly enough ; but his voice and
    his face were not kind,
And it was but a hopeless case, he had seen it and made
    up his mind,
And he said to me roughly, "The lad will need little
    more of your care."
"All the more need," I told him, "to seek the Lord
    Jesus in prayer ;
They are all His children here, and I pray for them all as
    my own :"
But he turn'd to me, "Ay, good woman, can prayer set
    a broken bone ?"
Then he mutter'd half to himself, but I knew that I
    heard him say,
"All very well—but the good Lord Jesus has had his
    day."

III.

Had ? has it come ? It has only dawn'd. It will come
    by and by.
O how could I serve in the wards if the hope of the
    world were a lie ?
How could I bear with the sights and the loathsome
    smells of disease
But that He said—"Ye do it to Me, when ye do it to
    these ?"

IV.

So he went. And we past to this ward where the
    younger children are laid :
Here is the cot of our orphan, our darling, our meek
    little maid ;

Empty you see just now! We have lost her who loved
    her so much—
Patient of pain—tho' as quick as a sensitive plant to the
    touch;
Hers was the prettiest prattle, it often moved me to
    tears,
Hers was the gratefullest heart I have found in a child
    of her years—
Nay, you remember our Emmie; you used to send her
    the flowers;
How she would smile at 'em, play with 'em, talk to 'em
    hours after hours;
They that can wonder at will when the works of the
    Lord are reveal'd,
Little guess what joy can be got from a cowslip out of the
    field;
Flowers to these 'spirits in prison' are all they can know
    of the spring,
They freshen and sweeten the wards like the waft of an
    angel's wing;
And she lay with a flower in one hand and her thin hands
    crost on her breast—
Wan, but as pretty as heart can desire, and we thought
    her at rest,
Quietly sleeping—so quiet, our doctor said "Poor little
    dear,
Nurse, I must do it to-morrow; she'll never live thro' it,
    I fear."

v.

I walk'd with our kindly old doctor as far as the head of
    the stair,
Then I return'd to the ward; the child didn't see I was
    there.

VI.

Never since I was a nurse had I been so grieved and so
    vext !
Emmie had heard him.   Softly she call'd from her cot
    to the next,
"He says I shall never live through it ; O Annie, what
    shall I do?"
Annie considered. "If I," said the wise little Annie,
    "was you,
I should cry to the dear Lord Jesus to help me, for
    Emmie, you see,   .
It's all in the picture there, ' Little children should come
    to Me ! ' "
(Meaning, the print that you gave us, I find that it
    always can please
Our children, the dear Lord Jesus with children about
    His knees).
"Yes, and I will," said Emmie, "but then if I call to
    the Lord,
How should He know that it's me? such a lot of beds in
    the ward ! "
That was a puzzle for Annie.   Again she consider'd and
    said—
"Emmie, you put out your arms, and you leave 'em
    outside on the bed—
The Lord has so *much* to see to ! but, Emmie, you tell it
    Him plain,
It's the little girl with her arms lying out on the counter-
    pane."

VII.

I had sat three nights by the child—I could not watch
    her for four—
My brain had begun to reel—I felt I could do it no more,

That was my sleeping night, but I thought that it never
would pass.
There was a thunder-clap once, and a clatter of hail on
the glass,
And there was a phantom cry that I heard as I tost
about,
The motherless bleat of a lamb in the storm and the
darkness without ;
My sleep was broken besides with dreams of the dreadful
knife,
And fears for our delicate Emmie who scarce could escape
with her life ;
Then in the gray of the morning it seem'd she stood by
me and smiled,
And the doctor came at his hour, and we went to see to
the child.

VIII.

He had brought his ghastly tools : we believed her asleep
again—
Her dear, long, lean little arms lying out on the counterpane ;
Say that this day is done ! Ah, why should we care what
they say ?
The Lord of the children had heard her, and Emmie had
passed away.

Lord Tennyson.

WEE WILLIE WINKIE.

WEE Willie Winkie rins through the toon,
Upstairs and downstairs in his nicht-gown,
Tirlin' at the window, crying at the lock,
"Are the weans in their bed, for it's now ten o'clock?"

"Hey, Willie Winkie, are ye comin' ben?
The cat's singing grey thrums to the sleepin' hen,
The dog's speldert on the floor, and disna gie a cheep,
But here's a waukrife laddie that wunna fa' asleep!

"Onything but sleep, you rogue! glow'ring like the
      moon,
Rattlin' in an airn jug wi' an airn spoon,
Rumblin', tumblin', roon about, crawin' like a cock,
Skirlin' like I kenna what, wauk'nin' sleepin' folk.

"Hey, Willie Winkie—the wean's in a creel!
Wamblin' aff a bodie's knee like a verra eel,
Ruggin' at the cat's lug, and ravelin' a' her thrums—
Hey, Willie Winkie—see, there he comes!"

Wearit is the mither that has a stoorie wean,
A wee stumpie stousie, that canna rin his lane,
That has a battle aye wi' sleep afore he'll close an e'e—
But a kiss frae aff his rosy lips gies strength anew to
      me.

                                        William Miller.

SPRING.

THE Spring comes linkin' and jinkin' through the
    wuds,
Openin' wi' gentle hand the bonnie green and yellow
    buds—
There's flowers an' showers, and sweet sang o' little bird,
An' the gowan wi' his red croon peepin' through the
    yird.

The hail comes rattlin' and brattlin' snell an' keen,
Daudin' and blaudin', tho' red set the sun at e'en ;
In bonnet an' wee loof the weans kep an' look for mair,
Dancin' thro'ither wi' the white pearls shinin' in their
    hair.

We meet wi' blythesome and kythesome cheerie weans,
Daffin' an' laughin' far adoon the leafy lanes,
Wi' gowans and buttercups buskin' the thorny wands—
Sweetly singin' wi' the flower-branch wavin' in their
    hands.

'Boon a' that's in thee, to win me, sweet Spring—
Bricht clouds an' green buds, and sangs that the birdies
    sing—
Flow'r-dappled hill-side, and dewy beech sae fresh at e'en—
Or the tappie-toorie fir-tree shining a' in green—

Bairnies bring treasure and pleasure mair to me—
Stealin' an' speilin' up to fondle on my knee !—
In spring-time the young things are bloomin' sae fresh
    and fair,
That I canna, Spring, but bless thee and love thee ever·
    mair.

                              William Miller.

THE WONDERFU' WEAN.

OUR wean's the most wonderfu' wean e'er I saw,
It would tak me a lang summer day to tell a'
His pranks, frae the morning, till night shuts his e'e,
When he sleeps like a peerie, 'tween father and me.
For in his quiet turns, siccan questions he'll spier :—
How the moon can stick up in the sky that's sae clear ?
What gars the wind blaw ? and whar frae comes the rain ?
He's a perfect divèrt—he's a wonderfu' wean.

Or wha was the first bodie's father ? and wha
Made the very first snaw-shower that ever did fa' ?
And wha made the first bird that sang on a tree ?
And the water that sooms a' the ships in the sea ?—
But after I've told him as weel as I ken,
Again he begins wi' his wha ? and his when ?
And he looks aye sae watchfu' the while I explain,—
He's as auld as the hills—he's an auld-farrant wean.

And folk who hae skill o' the bumps on the head,
Hint there's mae ways than toiling o' winning ane's bread ;
How he'll be a rich man, and hae men to work for him,
Wi' a kyte like a bailie's, shug shugging afore him ;
Wi' a face like the moon, sober, sonsy, and douce,
And a back, for its breadth, like the side o' a house.
'Tweel I'm unco' ta'en up wi't, they make a' sae plain ;
He's just a town's talk—he's a by-ord'nar wean.

I ne'er can forget sic a laugh as I gat,
To see him put on father's waistcoat and hat ;
Then the lang-leggit boots gaed sae far ower his knees,
The tap loops wi' his fingers he grippit wi' ease,

Then he march'd thro' the house—he march'd but, he
    march'd ben,
Like ower many mae o' our great-little men,
That I leuch clean outright, for I couldna contain,
He was sic a conceit—sic an ancient-like wean.

But 'mid a' his daffin', sic kindness he shows,
That he's dear to my heart as the dew to the rose :
And the unclouded hinnie-beam aye in his e'e
Mak's him every day dearer and dearer to me.
Though fortune be saucy, and dorty, and dour,
And gloom through her fingers, like hills through a
    shower,
When bodies hae got a bit bairn o' their ain,
How he cheers up their hearts—he's the wonderfu' wean !

William Miller.

HAIRST.

Tho' weel I lo'e the budding Spring,
    I'll no misca' John Frost,
Nor will I roose the summer days
    At gowden autumn's cost ;
For a' the seasons in their turn
    Some wished-for pleasures bring,
And hand in hand they jink about,
    Like weans at jingo-ring.

For weel I mind how aft ye said,
    When winter nights were lang,
" I weary for the summer woods,
    The lintie's tittering sang."

But when the woods grew gay and green,
  And birds sang sweet and clear,
It then was, When will hairst-time come,
  The gloaming o' the year?

Oh ! hairst-time's like a lipping cup
  That's gi'en wi' furthy glee !
The fields are fu' o' yellow corn,
  Red apples bend the tree;
The genty air, sae ladylike !
  Has on a scented gown,
And wi' an airy string she leads
  The thistle-seed balloon.

The yellow corn will porridge mak',
  The apples taste your mou' ;
And ower the stibble rigs I'll chase
  The thistle-down wi' you ;
I'll pu' the haw frae aff the thorn,
  The red hip frae the brier—
For wealth hangs in each tangled nook
  In the gloaming o' the year.

Sweet Hope ! ye biggit hae a nest
  Within my bairnie's breast—
Oh ! may his tingling heart ne'er trow
  That whiles ye sing in jest ;
Some coming joys are dancing aye
  Before his langing cen,
He sees the flower that isna blown,
  And birds that ne'er were seen :—

The stibble rig is aye ahin' !
  The gowden grain afore,
And apples drap into his lap,
  Or row in at the door !

Come hairst-time, then, unto my bairn !
　Drest in your gayest gear,
Wi' saft and winnowing win's to cool
　The gloaming o' the year.

William Miller.

NEIGHBOUR NELLY.

I'M in love with neighbour Nelly,
　Though I know she's only ten,
While, alas ! I'm eight-and-forty,—
　And the marriedest of men !
I've a wife who weighs me double,
　I've three daughters all with beaux ;
I've a son with noble whiskers,
　Who at me turns up his nose—

Though a square-toes, and a fogey,
　Still I've sunshine in my heart :
Still I'm fond of cakes and marbles,
　Can appreciate a tart—
I can love my neighbour Nelly
　Just as tho' I were a boy :
I could hand her nuts and apples
　From my depths of corduroy.

She is tall, and growing taller,
　She is vigorous of limb:
(You should see her play at cricket
　With her little brother Jim.)
She has eyes as blue as damsons,
　She has pounds of auburn curls,
She regrets the game of leap-frog
　Is prohibited to girls.

I adore my neighbour Nelly,
   I invite her in to tea :
And I let her nurse the baby—
   All her pretty ways to see.
Such a darling bud of woman,
   Yet remote from any teens,—
I have learnt from baby Nelly
   What the girl's doll instinct means.

Oh ! to see her with the baby !
   He adores her more than I,—
How she choruses his crowing,—
   How she hushes every cry !
How she loves to pit his dimples
   With her light forefinger deep,
How she boasts to me in triumph,
   When she's got him off to sleep !

We must part, my neighbour Nelly,
   For the summers quickly flee ;
And your middle-aged admirer
   Must supplanted quickly be.
Yet as jealous as a mother,—
   A distemper'd canker'd churl,
I look vainly for the setting
   To be worthy such a pearl.

                    Robert B. Brough.

THE MOTHER'S DREAM.

I'D a dream to-night
As I fell asleep,
Oh ! the touching sight
Makes me still to weep—
Of my little lad,
Soon to leave me sad,
Aye, the child I had,
But was not to keep.

As in heaven high,
I my child did seek,
There, in train, came by
Children fair and meek,
Each in lily white,
With a lamp alight ;
Each was clear to sight,
But they did not speak.

Then, a little sad,
Came my child in turn,
But the lamp he had,
Oh ! it did not burn ;
He, to clear my doubt,
Said, half turned about,
"Your tears put it out ;
Mother, never mourn."

William Barnes.

THE CHILD LOST.

WHEN evening is closing in all round,
And winds in the dark bough'd timber sound,
The flame of my candle, dazzling bright,
May shine full clear—full clear may shine,
But never can show my child to sight.

And warm is the bank, where boughs are still,
On timber below the windward hill,
But now, in the stead of summer hay,
Dead leaves are cast—are cast dead leaves,
Where lately I saw my child at play.

And oh ! could I see, as may be known
To angels, my little maid full grown,
As times would have made her, woman tall,
If she had lived—if lived had she,
And not have died now, so young and small.

Do children that go to heaven play?
Are young that were gay, in heaven gay?
Are old people bow'd by weak'ning time,
In heaven bow'd,—all bow'd in heaven?
Or else are they all in blissful prime?

Yes, blest with all blessings are the blest,
Their lowest of good's above the best,
So show me the highest soul you can
In shape and mind—in mind and shape,
Yet far above him is heaven's man.

William Barnes.

THE GYPSY GIRL.

PASSING I saw her as she stood beside
A lonely stream between two barren wolds;
Her loose vest hung in rudely-gathered folds
On her swart bosom, which in maiden pride
Pillowed a string of pearls; among her hair
Twined the light blue-bell and the stone-crop gay;
And not far thence the small encampment lay,
Curling its wreathèd smoke into the air.
She seemed a child of some sun-favoured clime;
So still, so habited to warmth and rest;
And in my wayward musings on past time,
When my thought fills with treasured memories,
That image nearest borders on the blest
Creations of pure art that never dies.

Henry Alford.

EPIMENIDES.

HE went into the woods a laughing boy;
Each flower was in his heart; the happy bird
Flitting across the morning sun, or heard
From wayside thicket, was to him a joy:
The water-springs that in their moist employ
Leapt from their banks, with many an inward word
Spoke to his soul, and every bird that stirred
Found notice from his quickly-glancing eye.
There wondrous sleep fell on him; many a year
His lids were closed: youth left him and he woke
A careful noter of men's ways; of clear
And lofty spirit: sages, when he spoke,
Forgot their systems; and the worldly-wise
Shrunk from the gaze of truth with baffled eyes.

Henry Alford.

THE HERD LADDIE.

It's a lang time yet till the kye gae hame,
It's a weary time yet till the kye gae hame:
Till lang shadows fa' in the sun's yellow flame,
And the birds sing gude-nicht, as the kye gae hame.

Sair langs the herd laddie for gloamin's sweet fa',
But slow moves the sun to the hills far awa';
In the shade and the broom-bush how fain would he lie,
But there's nae rest for him when he's herding the kye.

They'll no be content wi' the grass on the lea,
For do what he will to the corn aye they'll be;
The weary wee herd laddie to pity there is nane,
Sae tired and sae hungry wi' herding his lane.

When the bee's in its byke, and the bird in its nest,
And the kye in the byre, that's the hour he lo'es best;
Wi' a fu' cog o' brose he sleeps like a stane,—
But it scarce seems a blink till he's wauken'd again.

Alexander Smart.

THE TRUANT.

Wee Sandy in the corner
　　Sits greeting on a stool,
And sair the laddie rues
　　Playing truant frae the school;
Then ye'll learn frae silly Sandy,
　　Wha's gotten sic a fright,
To do naething through the day
　　That may gar ye greet at night.

He durstna venture hame now,
　Nor play, though e'er so fine,
And ilka ane he met wi'
　He thought them sure to ken,
And started at ilk whin bush,
　Though it was braid daylight—
Sae do naething through the day
　That may gar ye greet at night.

Wha winna be advised
　Are sure to rue ere lang;
And muckle pains it costs them
　To do the thing that's wrang,
When they wi' half the fash o't
　Might aye be in the right,
And do naething through the day
　That would gar them greet at night.

What fools are wilfu' bairns,
　Who misbehave frae hame!
There's something in the breast aye
　That tells them they're to blame;
And then when comes the gloamin',
　They're in a waefu' plight!
Sae do naething through the day
　That may gar ye greet at night.

Alexander Smart.

OF ME!

OUR grandsire poets often prayed
All the nine Muses to their aid!
　But I, who only wander round
　Familiar ground,

By pleasant autumn hedges bound,—
    Sure I can pray
For inspiration much more near ;
    My audience dear,
Assist me to a theme to-day !

You cannot help me ? but I see
I have a readier prompter here,
The child is whispering in my ear,
" Write a pretty thing of me."
I will, you egotistic gnome,
The best is often nearest home.

LITTLE BOY.

I.

LITTLE boy, whose great round eye
Hath the tincture of the sky,
    Answer now, and tell me true,
Whence and what and why are you ?
And he answered,—" Mother's boy."
      Yes, yes, I know,
      But 'twas not so
      Six years ago.
You are mother's anxious joy,
      Mother's pet,
      But yet—
A trouble came within the eye
That had some tincture of the sky.

II.

I looked again, within that eye
    There was a question, not reply—
    I only shaded back his hair,
And kissed him there ;

But from that day
There was more thinking and less play;
   And that round eye,
That had a tincture of the sky,
Was somewhat shaded in its sheen ;
It looked and listened far away,
As if for what can not be seen.

III.

When I turned about and cried,
   But who am I,
Prompting thus the dawning soul?
   I cannot hide
   The want of a reply,
Though travelling nearer to the goal,
Where we take no note of time :
I can only say I AM,
A phrase, a word, that hath no rhyme,
The name God called Himself, the best
To answer the weak patriarch's guest.

IV.

"Why talk nonsense to the child?"
   Asks the mother from the fire,
   Listening through both back and ears,
Listening with a mother's fears :—
"Already is he something wild,
Says that he can fly downstair !
   I do desire
You questioning men would have a care,—
He is my child, my only one,
You'll make him try to touch the sun !"

William Bell Scott.

PIPPA'S SONG.

OVERHEAD the tree-tops meet,
Flowers and grass spring 'neath one's feet;
There was nought above me, nought below,
My childhood had not learned to know:
For, what are the voices of birds
—Aye, and of beasts,—but words, our words,
Only so much more sweet?
The knowledge of that with my life begun.
But I had so near made out the sun,
And counted your stars, the seven and one,
Like the fingers of my hand:
Nay, I could all but understand
Wherefore through heaven the white moon ranges;
And just when out of her soft fifty changes
No unfamiliar face might overlook me—
Suddenly God took me.

Robert Browning.

THE BOY AND THE ANGEL.

MORNING, evening, noon, and night,
" Praise God ! " sang Theocrite.

Then to his poor trade he turned,
Whereby the daily meal was earned.

Hard he laboured, long and well;
O'er his work the boy's curls fell.

But ever, at each period,
He stopped and sang, " Praise God ! "

Then back again his curls he threw,
And cheerfully turned to work anew.

Said Blaise, the listening monk, " Well done ;
I doubt not thou art heard, my son :

As well as if thy voice to-day
Were praising God, the Pope's great way.

This Easter Day, the Pope at Rome
Praises God from Peter's dome."

Said Theocrite, "Would God that I
Might praise Him that great way, and die !"

Night passed, day shone,
And Theocrite was gone.

With God a day endures alway,
A thousand years are but a day.

God said in heaven, " Nor day nor night
Now brings the voice of my delight."

Then Gabriel, like a rainbow's birth,
Spread his wings and sank to earth ;

Entered, in flesh, the empty cell,
Lived there, and played the craftsman well ;

And morning, evening, noon, and night,
Praised God in place of Theocrite.

And from a boy to youth he grew:
The man put off the stripling's hue:

The man matured and fell away
Into the season of decay:

And even o'er the trade he bent,
And ever lived on earth content.

(He did God's will; to him all one
If on the earth or in the sun.)

God said, " A praise is in mine ear;
There is no doubt in it, no fear:

So sing old worlds, and so
New worlds that from my footstool go.

Clearer loves sound other ways:
I miss my little human praise."

Then forth sprang Gabriel's wings, off fell
The flesh disguise, remained the cell.

'Twas Easter Day: he flew to Rome,
And paused above St. Peter's dome.

In the tiring room close by
The great outer gallery,

With his holy vestments dight
Stood the new Pope, Theocrite:

And all his past career
Came back upon him clear,

Since when, a boy, he plied his trade,
Till on his life the sickness weighed;

And in his cell when death drew near,
An angel in a dream brought cheer :

And rising from the sickness drear,
He grew a priest, and now stood here.

To the east with praise he turned,
And on his sight the angel burned.

"I bore thee from thy craftsman's cell,
And set thee here ; I did not well.

Vainly I left my angel-sphere,
Vain was thy dream of many a year.

Thy voice's praise seemed weak ; it dropped—
Creation's chorus stopped !

Go back and praise again
The early way, while I remain.

With that weak voice of our disdain,
Take up Creation's pausing strain.

Back to the cell and poor employ :
Resume the craftsman and the boy ! "

Theocrite grew old at home ;
A new Pope dwelt in Peter's dome.

One vanished as the other died ;
They sought God side by side.

Robert Browning.

31

PROTUS.

AMONG these latter busts we count by scores,
Half-emperors and quarter emperors,
Each with his bay-leaf fillet, loose-thonged vest,
Loric and low-crowned Gorgon on the breast,—
One loves a baby face, with violets there,
Violets instead of laurel in the hair,
As those were all the little locks could bear.

Now read here.   " Protus ends a period
Of empery beginning with a god ;
Born in the porphyry chamber at Byzant,
Queens by his cradle, proud and ministrant :
And if he quickened breath there, 'twould like fire
Pantingly through the dim vast realm transpire.
A fame that he was missing, spread afar :
The world, from its four corners, rose in war,
Till he was borne out on a balcony
To pacify the world when it should see.

The captains ranged before him ; one his hand
Made baby points at, gained the chief command.
And day by day more beautiful he grew
In shape, all said, in features and in hue,
While young Greek sculptors gazing on the child
Became with old Greek sculpture reconciled.
Already sages laboured to condense
In easy tomes a life's experience :
And artists took grave counsel to impart
In one breath and one hand-sweep, all their art—
To make his graces prompt as blossoming
Of plentifully-watered palms in spring :

Since well beseems it, whoso mounts the throne,
For beauty, knowledge, strength, should stand alone,
And mortals love the letters of his name. "

—Stop ! Have you turned two pages ? Still the same.
New reign, same date. The scribe goes on to say
How that same year, on such a month and day,
"John the Pannonian, groundedly believed
A blacksmith's bastard, whose hard hand reprieved
The Empire from its fate the year before,—
Came, had a mind to take the crown, and wore
The same for six years (during which the Huns
Kept off their fingers from us) till his sons
Put something in his liquor "—and so forth.
Then a new reign. Stay—"Take at its just worth,"
(Subjoins an annotator) " what I give
As hearsay. Some think, John let Protus live
And slip away. 'Tis said he reached man's age
At some blind northern court ; made, first a page,
Then tutor to the children ; last of use
About the hunting stables. I deduce
He wrote the little tract 'On worming dogs,'
Whereof the name in sundry catalogues
Is extant yet. A Protus of the race
Is rumoured to have died a monk in Thrace,—
And if the same, he reached senility."

Here's John the Smith's rough-hammered head.
    Great eye,
Gross jaw, and griped lip do what granite can
To give you the crown-grasper. What a man !

Robert Browning.

ZOE, AN ATHENIAN CHILD.

I.

BLUE eyes, but of so dark a blue
That sadder souls than mine
Find nought but night beneath their dew,—
Such locks as Proserpine
Around her shadowy forehead wears,
Made smoother by Elysian airs,
And lips whose song spontaneous swells
Like airs from Ocean's moonlit shells—
These, lovely child ! are thine ;
And that forlorn yet radiant grace
That best becomes thy name and race !

II.

A forehead orbèd with the light ;
Pure temples marbled round
By feathery veins that streak the white,
More white thus dimly wound,
And taper fingers, hands self-folded,
Like shapes of alabaster moulded,
And cheek whose blushes are as those
Aurora cools on Pindar snows
Ere night is yet discrowned—
Not brighter, clad in Fancy's hues,
Or seen in dream—an Infant Muse.

III.

O fetch her from yon Naxian glade
One chaplet of the Bacchic vine,
Or glimmering ivy-wreath yet sprayed
With dews that taste like wine !

She loves to pace the wild sea-shore—
Or drop her wandering fingers o'er
The bosom of some chorded shell :
Her touch will make it speak as well
As infant Hermes made
That tortoise, in its own despite
Thenceforth in Heaven a shape star-bright !
Aubrey de Vere.

A CONVENT SCHOOL IN A CORRUPT CITY.

HARK how they laugh, those children at their sport !
O'er all this city vast that knows not sleep
Labour and sin their ceaseless vigil keep :
Yet hither still good angels make resort.
Innocence here and Mirth a single fort
Maintain : and though in many a snake-like sweep
Corruption round the weedy walls doth creep,
Its track not yet hath slimed this sunny court.
Glory to God, who so the world hath framed
That in all places children more abound
Than they by whom Humanity is shamed !
Children outnumber men : and millions die—
Who knows not this ?—in blameless infancy
Sowing with innocence our sin-stained ground.
Aubrey de Vere.

MY DARLINGS.

WHEN steps are hurrying homeward,
    And night the world o'erspreads,
And I see at the open windows
    The shining of little heads,
I think of you, my darlings,
    In your low and lonesome beds.

And when the latch is lifted,
  And I hear the voices glad,
I feel my arms more empty,
  My heart more widely sad ;
For we measure dearth of blessings
  By the blessings we have had.

But sometimes in sweet visions
  My faith to sight expands,
And with my babes in his bosom
  My Lord before me stands,
And I feel on my head bowed lowly
  The touches of little hands.

Then pain is lost in patience,
  And tears no longer flow :
They are only dead to the sorrow
  And sin of life, I know ;
For if they were not immortal,
  My love would make them so.

                      Alice Cary.

ADELIED.

UNPRAISED but of my simple rhymes,
  She pined from life and died,
The softest of all April times
  That storm and shine divide.

The swallow twittered within reach,
  Impatient of the rain,
And the red blossoms of the peach
  Blew down against the pane.

When, feeling that life's wasting sands
    Were wearing into hours,
She took her long locks in her hands,
    And gathered out the flowers.

The day was nearly on the close,
    And on the eave in sight
The doves were gathered in white rows,
    With bosoms to the light:

When first my sorrow flowed to rhymes
    For gentle Adelied—
The light of thrice five April times
    Had kissed her when she died.

                    Alice Cary.

MY BOYHOOD.

AH me! those joyous days are gone!
I little dreamt, till they were flown,
    How fleeting were the hours!
For, lest he break the pleasing spell,
Time bears for youth a muffled bell,
    And hides his face in flowers!

Ah! well I mind me of the days,
Still bright in memory's fluttering rays,
    When all was fair and new;
When knaves were only found in books,
And friends were known by friendly looks,
    And love was always true!

While yet of sin I scarcely dreamed,
And everything was what it seemed,
    And all too bright for choice;
When fays were wont to guard my sleep,
And *Crusoe* still could make me weep,
    And *Santa Claus*, rejoice!

When heaven was pictured to my thought
(In spite of all my mother taught
    Of happiness serene)
A theatre of boyish plays—
One glorious round of holidays,
    Without a school between!

Ah me! those joyous days are gone!
I little dreamt, till they were flown,
    How fleeting were the hours!
For, lest he break the pleasing spell,
Time bears for youth a muffled bell,
    And hides his face in flowers!

                  John Godfrey Saxe.

THERE WAS A CHILD WENT FORTH.

THERE was a child went forth every day;
And the first object he looked upon, that object he
    became;
And that object became part of him for the day, or a
    certain part of the day, or for many years, or stretch-
    ing cycles of years.

The early lilacs became part of this child,
And grass, and white and red " morning-glories," and
white and red clover, and the song of the phœbe-
bird,
And the Third-month lambs, and the sow's pink-faint
litter, and the mare's foal, and the cow's calf,
And the noisy brood of the barn-yard, or by the mire of
the pond-side,
And the fish suspending themselves so curiously below
there—and the beautiful curious liquid,
And the water-plants with their graceful flat heads—all
became part of him.

The field-sprouts of Fourth-month and Fifth-month
became part of him ;
Winter-grain sprouts, and those of the light-yellow corn,
and the esculent roots of the garden,
And the apple-trees covered with blossoms, and the fruit
afterward, and wood-berries, and the commonest
weeds by the road ;
And the old drunkard staggering home from the out-
house of the tavern, whence he had lately risen,
And the schoolmistress that passed on her way to the
school,
And the friendly boys that passed—and the quarrelsome
boys,
And the tidy and fresh-cheeked girls—and the bare-foot
negro boy and girl,
And all the changes of city and country, wherever he
went.

His own parents,
He that had fathered him, and she that had conceived
him in her womb, and birthed him,

They gave this child more of themselves than that ;
They gave him afterward every day—they became part
  of him.

The mother at home, quietly placing the dishes on the
  supper-table ;
The mother with mild words—clean her cap and gown,
  a wholesome odour falling off her person and clothes
  as she walks by ;
The father, strong, self-sufficient, manly, mean, angered,
  unjust ;
The blow, the quick loud word, the tight bargain, the
  crafty lure,
The family usages, the language, the company, the fur-
  niture—the yearning and swelling heart,
Affection that will not be gainsaid—the sense of what is
  real—the thought if, after all, it should prove unreal,
The doubts of day-time and the doubts of night-time—
  the curious whether and how,
Whether that which appears so is so, or is it all flashes
  and specks?
Men and women crowding fast in the streets—if they are
  not flashes and specks, what are they?
The streets themselves, and the façades of houses, and
  goods in the windows,
Vehicles, teams, the heavy-planked wharves—the huge
  crossing at the ferries,
The village on the highland, seen from afar at sunset—
  the river between,
Shadows, aureola and mist, the light falling on roofs and
  gables of white or brown, three miles off,
The schooner near by, sleepily dropping down the tide
  —the little boat slack-towed astern,
The hurrying tumbling waves quick-broken crests slap-
  ping,

The strata of coloured clouds, the long bar of maroon-
tint, away solitary by itself—the spread of purity it
lies motionless in,
The horizon's edge, the flying sea-crow, the fragrance of
salt marsh and shore-mud ;
These became part of that child who went forth every
day, and who now goes, and will always go forth
every day.

Walt Whitman.

THE CHANGELING.

I HAD a little daughter,
  And she was given to me
To lead me gently backward
  To the Heavenly Father's knee,
That I, by the force of nature,
  Might in some dim wise divine
The depth of His infinite patience
  To this wayward soul of mine.

I know not how others saw her,
  But to me she was wholly fair,
And the light of the heaven she came from
  Still lingered and gleamed in her hair;
For it was as wavy and golden,
  And as many changes took
As the shadows of sun-gilt ripples
  On the yellow bed of a brook.

To what can I liken her smiling
  Upon me, her kneeling lover,
How it leaped from her lips to her eyelids,
  And dimpled her wholly over,

Till her outstretched hands smiled also,
  And I almost seemed to see
The very heart of her mother
  Sending sun through her veins to me !

She had been with us scarce a twelvemonth,
  And it hardly seemed a day,
When a troop of wandering angels
  Stole my little daughter away ;
Or perhaps those heavenly Zingari
  But loosed the hampering strings,
And when they had opened her cage-door,
  My little bird used her wings.

But they left in her stead a changeling,
  A little angel child,
That seems like her bud in full blossom,
  And smiles as she never smiled :
When I wake in the morning, I see it
  Where she always used to lie,
And I feel as weak as a violet
  Alone 'neath the awful sky ;

As weak, yet as trustful also ;
  For the whole year long I see
All the wonders of faithful Nature
  Still worked for the love of me ;
Winds wander, and dews drip earthward,
  Rain falls, suns rise and set,
Earth whirls, and all but to prosper
  A poor little violet.

This child is not mine as the first was,
  I cannot sing it to rest,
I cannot lift it up fatherly
  And bless it upon my breast ;

Yet it lies in my little one's cradle
  And sits in my little one's chair,
And the light of the heaven she's gone to
  Transfigures its golden hair.

John Russell Lowell.

THE FIRST SNOW-FALL.

THE snow had begun in the gloaming,
  And busily all the night
Had been heaping field and highway
  With a silence deep and white.

Every pine and fir and hemlock
  Wore ermine too dear for an earl,
And the poorest twig on the elm-tree
  Was ridged inch-deep with pearl.

From sheds new-roofed with Carrara
  Came Chanticleer's muffled crow,
The stiff rails were softened to swans'-down,
  And still fluttered down the snow.

I stood and watched by the window
  The noiseless work of the sky,
And the sudden flurries of snow-birds,
  Like brown leaves whirling by.

I thought of a mound in sweet Auburn,
  Where a little headstone stood ;
How the flakes were folding it gently,
  As did robins the babes in the wood.

Up spoke our own little Mabel,
　Saying " Father, who makes it snow ? "
And I told of the good All-father
　Who cares for us here below.

Again I looked at the snow-fall,
　And thought of the leaden sky
That arched o'er our first great sorrow,
　When that mound was heaped so high.

I remembered the gradual patience
　That fell from that cloud like snow,
Flake by flake, healing and hiding
　The scar of our deep-plunged woe.

And again to the child I whispered,
　" The snow that husheth all,
Darling, the merciful Father
　Alone can make it fall ! "

Then, with eyes that saw not, I kissed her ;
　And she kissing back could not know
That *my* kiss was given to her sister,
　Folded close under deepening snow.

　　　　　　John Russell Lowell.

BROTHER AND SISTER.

I.

I CANNOT choose but think upon the time
When our two lives grew like two buds that kiss
At lightest thrill from the bee's swinging chime,
Because the one so near the other is.
He was the elder, and a little man
Of forty inches, bound to show no dread,
And I the girl that, puppy-like, now ran,
Now lagged behind my brother's larger tread.
I held him wise, and when he talked to me
Of snakes and birds, and which God loved the best,
I thought his knowledge marked the boundary
Where men grow blind, though angels knew the
    rest.
If he said " Hush ! " I tried to hold my breath ;
Whenever he said " Come ! " I stepped in faith.

II.

School parted us ; we never found again
That childish world where our two spirits mingled
Like scents from varying roses that remain
One sweetness, nor can evermore be singled ;
Yet the twin habit of that early time
Lingered for long about the heart and tongue :
We had been natives of one happy clime
And its dear accent to our utterance clung :
Till the dire years whose awful name is Change
Had grasped our souls still yearning in divorce.
And, pitiless, shaped them into two forms that range,
Two elements which sever their life's course.
But were another childhood world my share,
I would be born a little sister there.

George Eliot.

BABY MAY.

CHEEKS as soft as July peaches,
Lips whose dewy scarlet teaches
Poppies paleness—round large eyes
Ever great with new surprise,
Minutes fill'd with shadeless gladness,
Minutes just as brimm'd with sadness,
Happy smiles and wailing cries,
Crows and laughs and tearful eyes,
Lights and shadows swifter born
Than on windswept Autumn corn,
Ever some new tiny notion
Making every limb all motion—
Catchings up of legs and arms,
Throwings back and small alarms,
Clutching fingers—straightening jerks,
Twining feet whose each toe works,
Kickings up and straining risings,
Mother's ever new surprisings,
Hands all wants and looks all wonder
At all things the heavens under,
Tiny scorns of smiled reprovings
That have more of love than lovings,
Mischiefs done with such a winning
Archness, that we prize such sinning,
Breakings dire of plates and glasses,
Graspings small at all that passes,
Pullings off of all that's able
To be caught from tray or table.
Silences—small meditations
Deep as thoughts of cares for nations,
Breaking into wisest speeches
In a tongue that nothing teaches,

All the thoughts of whose possessing
Must be wooed to light by guessing ;
Slumbers—such sweet angel-seemings
That we'd ever have such dreamings,
Till from sleep we see thee breaking,
And we'd always have thee waking ;
Wealth for which we know no measure,
Pleasure high above all pleasure,
Gladness brimming over gladness,
Joy in care—delight in sadness,
Loveliness beyond completeness,
Sweetness distancing all sweetness,
Beauty all that beauty may be—
That's May Bennett—that's my baby.

W. Bennett.

A TERRIBLE INFANT.

I RECOLLECT a nurse called Ann,
    Who carried me about the grass,
And one fine day a fair young man
    Came up and kissed the pretty lass :
She did not make the least objection !
            Thinks I, *Aha !*
When I can talk I'll tell Mamma !
—And that's my earliest recollection.

Frederick Locker.

THE WIDOW'S MITE.

A WIDOW—she had only one !
A puny and decrepit son ;
    But, day and night,
Though fretful oft, and weak and small,
A loving child, he was her all—
    The Widow's Mite.

The Widow's Mite—ay, so sustain'd,
She battled onward, nor complain'd
    Tho' friends were fewer ;
And while she toiled for daily fare,
A little crutch upon the stair
    Was music to her.

I saw her then—and now I see
That, though resign'd and cheerful, she
    Has sorrow'd much :
She has, He gave it tenderly,
Much faith ; and, carefully laid by,
    A little crutch.

Frederick Locker.

A RHYME OF ONE.

You sleep upon your mother's breast,
    Your race begun,
A welcome, long and wished-for guest,
    Whose age is One.

A baby-boy, you wonder why
    You cannot run ;
You try to talk—how hard you try !—
    You're only One.

Ere long you won't be such a dunce ;
        You'll eat your bun
And fly your kite, like folk who once
        Were only One.

You'll rhyme, and woo, and fight, and joke,
        Perhaps you'll pun !
Such feats are never done by folk
        Before they're One.

Some day, too, you may have your joy,
        And envy none :
Yes, you, yourself, may own a boy
        Who isn't One.

He'll dance, and laugh, and crow, he'll do
        As you have done :
(You crown a happy home, though you
        Are only One).

But when he's grown shall you be here
        To share his fun,
And talk of times when he (the dear)
        Was hardly One ?

Dear child, 'tis your poor lot to be
        My little son ;
I'm glad, though I am old, you see—
        While you are One.
                Frederick Locker.

THE OLD CRADLE.

AND this was your Cradle? Why surely my Jenny,
  Such cosy dimensions go clearly to show,
You were an exceedingly small picaninny
  Some nineteen or twenty short summers ago.

Your baby-days flowed in a much-troubled channel,
    I see you as then, in your impotent strife,
A light little bundle of wailing and flannel,
    Perplexed with the newly found fardel of Life.

To hint at infantile frailty's a scandal ;
    Let bygones be bygones, for somebody knows
It was bliss such a baby to dance and to dandle,—
    Your cheeks were so dimpled, so rosy your toes.

Aye, here is your Cradle ; and Hope, a bright spirit,
    With Love now is watching beside it, I know.
They guard the wee nest it was yours to inherit
    Some nineteen or twenty short summers ago.

It is Hope gilds the future, Love welcomes it smiling ;
    Thus wags this old world, therefore stay not to ask,
" My future bids fair, is my future beguiling ? "
    If mask'd, still it pleases—then raise not its mask.

Is Life a poor coil some would gladly be doffing ?
    He is riding post haste who their wrongs will adjust ;
For at most it's a footstep from cradle to coffin—
    From a spoonful of pap to a mouthful of dust.

Then smile as your future is smiling, my Jenny ;
    I see you, except for those infantine woes,
Little changed since you were but a small picaninny—
    Your cheeks were so dimpled, so rosy your toes ;

Ay, here is the Cradle, much, much to my liking,
    Though nineteen or twenty long winters have sped.
Hark ! as I'm talking there's six o'clock striking,—
    It is time *Jenny's Baby* should be in its bed.

                                        Frederick Locker.

THE CHILDREN'S HEAVEN.

THE infant lies in blessed ease
　Upon his mother's breast ;
No storm, no dark, the baby sees
　Invade his heaven of rest.
He nothing knows of change or death—
　Her face his holy skies ;
The air he breathes, his mother's breath—
　His stars, his mother's eyes.

Yet half the sighs that wander there
　Are born of doubts and fears ;
The dew slow falling through that air—
　It is the dew of tears.
And ah ! my child, thy heavenly home
　Hath rain as well as dew ;
Black clouds fill sometimes all its dome,
　And quench the starry blue.

Her smile would win no smile again,
　If baby saw the things
That ache across his mother's brain,
　The while she sweetly sings.
Thy faith in us is faith in vain—
　We are not what we seem.
O dreary day, O cruel pain,
　That wakes thee from thy dream !

No ; pity not his dream so fair,
　Nor fear the waking grief ;
Oh, safer so than though we were
　Good as his vague belief !

There is a heaven that heaven above
   Whereon he gazes now ;
A truer love than in thy kiss ;
   A better friend than thou.

The father's arms fold like a nest
   His children round about ;
His face looks down, a heaven of rest,
   Where comes no dark, no doubt.
Its mists are clouds of stars that move
   In sweet concurrent strife ;
Its winds, the goings of his love ;
   Its dew, the dew of life.

We for our children seek thy heart,
   For them the Father's eyes :
Lord, when their hopes in us depart,
   Let hopes in thee arise.
When childhood's visions them forsake,
   To women grown and men,
Thou to thy heart their hearts wilt take,
   And bid them dream again.

              George Macdonald.

BABY.

WHERE did you come from, baby dear ?
Out of the everywhere into here.

Where did you get those eyes so blue ?
Out of the sky as I came through.

What makes the light in them sparkle and spin ?
Some of the starry spikes left in.

Where did you get that little tear?
I found it waiting when I got here.

What makes your forehead so smooth and high?
A soft hand stroked it as I went by.

What makes your cheek like a warm white rose?
I saw something better than any one knows.

Whence that three-cornered smile of bliss?
Three angels gave me at once a kiss.

Where did you get this pearly ear?
God spoke, and it came out to hear.

Where did you get those arms and hands?
Love made itself into bonds and bands.

Feet, whence did you come, you darling things?
From the same box as the cherub's wings.

How did they all just come to be you?
God thought about me, and so I grew.

But how did you come to us, you dear?
God thought about you, and so I am here.

George Macdonald.

THE TOYS.

My little Son, who look'd from thoughtful eyes,
And moved and spoke in quiet grown-up wise,
Having my law the seventh time disobey'd,
I struck him, and dismiss'd

With hard words and unkiss'd,
His mother, who was patient, being dead.
Then, fearing lest his grief should hinder sleep,
I visited his bed,
But found him slumbering deep,
With darken'd eyelids, and their lashes yet
From his late sobbing wet.
And I, with moan,
Kissing away his tears, left others of my own ;
For, on a table drawn beside his head,
He had put, within his reach,
A box of counters and a red-veined stone,
A piece of glass abraded by the beach,
And six or seven shells,
A bottle with bluebells,
And two French copper coins, ranged there with
    careful art
To content his sad heart.
So when that night I pray'd
To God, I wept, and said :
Ah, when at last we lie with trancèd breath,
Not vexing Thee in death,
And thou rememberest of what toys
We made our joys,
How weakly understood,
Thy great commanded good,
Then, fatherly not less
Than I whom Thou hast moulded from the clay,
Thou'lt leave Thy wrath, and say,
" I will be sorry for their childishness."

                          Coventry Patmore.

THE LITTLE GIRL'S SONG.

Do not mind my crying, Papa, I am not crying for
    pain,
Do not mind my shaking, Papa, I am not shaking
    with fear ;
Though the wild wind is hideous to hear,
    And I see the snow and the rain.
    When will you come back again,
        Papa, Papa ?

    Somebody else that you love, Papa,
Somebody else that you dearly love,
Is weary, like me, because you're away.
Sometimes I see her lips tremble and move,
And I seem to know what they're going to say ;
And every day, and all the long day,
I long to cry, " O Mama, Mama,
When will Papa come back again ? "

But before I can say it, I see the pain
Creeping up on her white, white cheek,
As the sweet sad sunshine creeps up the white wall,
And then I am sorry and fear to speak ;
And slowly the pain goes out of her cheek,
As the sad sweet sunshine goes from the wall.
Oh, I wish I were grown up wise and tall,
That I might throw my arms around her neck
And say, " Dear Mama, what is it all
That I see and see and do not see,
In your white, white face all the livelong day ? "
But she hides her grief from a child like me.
    When will you come back again,
        Papa, Papa ?

Where were you going, Papa, Papa?
All this long while have you been on the sea?
When she looks as if she saw far away,
Is she thinking of you, and what does she see?
    Are the white sails blowing,
    And the blue men rowing,
And are you standing on the high deck
Where we saw you stand till the ship grew grey,
And we watch'd and watch'd till the ship was a speck,
And the dark came first to you, far away?
I wish I could see what she can see,
But she hides her grief from a child like me.
    When will you come back again,
        Papa, Papa?

Don't you remember, Papa, Papa,
How we used to sit by the fire, all three,
And she told me tales while I sat on her knee,
And heard the winter winds roar down the street,
And knock like men at the window pane;
And the louder they roar, oh, it seemed more sweet
To be warm and warm as we used to be,
Sitting at night by the fire, all three.
    When will you come back again,
        Papa, Papa?

Papa, I like to sit by the fire:
Why does she sit far away in the cold?
If I had but somebody wise and old,
That every day I might cry and say,
"Is she changed, do you think, or do I forget?
Was she always as white as she is to-day?
Did she never carry her head up higher?"
Papa, Papa, if I could but know!
Do you think her voice was always so low?

Did I always see what I seem to see
When I wake up at night and her pillow is wet?
You used to say her hair it was gold—
It looks like silver to me.
But still she tells the same tale that she told,
She sings the same song when I sit on her knee,
And the hour goes on as it went long ago,
When we lived together, all three.
Sometimes my heart seems to sink, Papa,
And I feel as if I could be happy no more.
Is she changed, do you think, Papa,
Or did I dream she was brighter before?

    She makes me remember my snowdrop, Papa,
That I forgot in thinking of you,
The sweetest snowdrop that ever I knew!
But I put it out of the sun and the rain :
It was green and white when I put it away,
It had one sweet ball and green leaves four ;
It was green and white when I found it that day,
It had one pale ball and green leaves four,
But I was not glad of it any more.
Was it changed, do you think, Papa,
Or did I dream it was brighter before?

Do not mind my crying, Papa, I am not crying with
    pain,
Do not mind my shaking, Papa, I am not shaking
    with fear ;
Though the wild wind is hideous to hear,
    And I see the snow and the rain.
    When will you come back again,
        Papa, Papa?

                        Sydney Dobell.

GOD'S GIFTS.

God gave a gift to Earth :—a child,
Weak, innocent, and undefiled,
Opened its ignorant eyes and smiled.

It lay so helpless, so forlorn,
Earth took it coldly and in scorn,
Cursing the day when it was born.

She gave it first a tarnished name,
For heritage, a tainted fame,
Then cradled it in want and shame.

All influence of Good or Right,
All ray of God's most holy light,
She curtained closely from its sight.

Then turned her heart, her eyes away,
Ready to look again, the day
Its little feet began to stray.

In dens of guilt the baby played,
Where sin, and sin alone, was made
The law that all around obeyed.

With ready and obedient care
He learnt the tasks they taught him there ;
Black sin for lesson—oaths for prayer.

The earth arose, and, in her might,
To vindicate her injured right,
Thrust him in deeper depths of night.

Branding him with a deeper brand
Of shame, he could not understand,
The felon outcast of the land.

———

God gave a gift to Earth :—a child,
Weak, innocent, and undefiled,
Opened its ignorant eyes and smiled.

And Earth received the gift, and cried
Her joy and triumph far and wide,
Till echo answered to her pride.

She blest the hour when first he came
To take the crown of pride and fame,
Wreathed through long ages for his name ;

Then bent her utmost art and skill
To train the supple mind and will,
And guard it from a breath of ill.

She strewed his morning path with flowers,
And Love, in tender drooping showers,
Nourished the blue and dawning hours.

She shed, in rainbow hues of light,
A halo round the Good and Right,
To tempt and charm the baby's sight.

And every step, of work or play,
Was lit by some such dazzling ray,
Till morning brightened into day.

And then the World arose, and said—
Let added honours now be shed
On such a noble heart and head !

O World, both gifts were pure and bright,
Holy and sacred in God's sight :—
God will judge them and thee aright !

Adelaide Ann Procter.

THE PAINTED WINDOW.

THIS is our painted window,
  Of pure white lights before,
But when my lord died, Lady Ann,
  To prove the love she bore,
Raised this, and turned his hunters out
  To grass for evermore.

And here she sits, beneath it,
  In amethyst and rose ;
And if the Virgin's kirtle
  Tinges her steadfast nose,
She heeds it not, but lurid
  Through Morning Service goes.

To see our famous window
  From all the country side,
The wondering rustics gather,
  And noise it far and wide ;
Till Lady Ann esteems it
  Our village boast and pride.

For me—I loved that better
　Which as a boy I knew,
Rearing its open arches
　Against God's solemn blue ;
Five portals which His glory
　Was ever streaming through.

Hour after hour beneath it
　The dreaming boy would sit,
And watch it, with the splendour
　Of Heaven's radiance lit—
A window beautiful indeed,
　For God had painted it !

Sometimes of the Good Shepherd
　Our loving pastor told,
And of the sheep He tended
　And, lo ! I saw the fold,
There in the blue reposing
　Cloud-white, or fleeced in gold.

Sometimes a sea of crystal
　The cloud-isles' rosy tips
Flushed through, or golden branches
　Waved over cloudy ships ;
And I beheld the vision
　Of John's Apocalypse.

The yew-tree's ragged branches
　Stretched black against the light ;
And when the stormy sunset
　Burned in it redly bright,
The burning bush on Horeb
　Gleam'd on my wond'ring sight.

And sometimes in the twilight,
  Before the prayer was done,
Out of the cooling opal
  The stars broke one by one :
To me they were the symbols
  Of Heaven's benizon.

So in each prayer repeated,
  Each sacred lesson taught,
'Twas Heaven itself assisted
  To shape the heavenly thought,
And on *my* painted window
  The holy picture wrought.

But now the pallid Virgin,
  With saffron-oozing hair,
For ever weeps, and ever
  The Four are rigid there :
And gold, and reds, and purples
  Are all their saintly wear.

The lights are mediæval,
  The figures square and quaint ;
But more I loved the splendour
  No human hand could paint—
The heav'n now darkened under
  Each intercepting saint.

As these were men, their presence
  Can all my manhood move,
Their sufferings all my pity,
  Their loving all my love :
But thoughts of men tend downward,
  And thoughts of God above.

And, as I am but human,
  Is this a gain to me?
To bound my soul's perceptions
  By their humanity?
To gaze upon God's sainted,
  Where God was wont to be?

William Sawyer.

MONSIEUR ET MADEMOISELLE.

DEUX petits enfants Français:
  Monsieur et Mademoiselle.
Of what can they be talking, child?
  Indeed I cannot tell.
But of this I am very certain,
  You would find naught to blame
In that sweet French politeness—
  I wish we had the same!

Monsieur has got a melon,
  And scoops it with his knife,
While Mademoiselle sits watching him:
  No rudeness here—or strife:
Though could you only listen,
  They're chattering like two pies—
French magpies, understand me—
  So merry and so wise.

Their floor is bare of carpet,
  Their curtains are so thin;
They dine off meagre potage, and
  Put many an onion in!

33

Her snow-white caps she irons ;
   He blacks his shoes, he can ;
Yet she's a little lady,
   And he a gentleman.

O busy, happy children
   That light French heart of yours,
Would it might sometimes enter at
   Our solemn English doors !
Would that we worked as gaily,
   And played, yes, played as well,
And lived our lives as simply
   As Monsieur and Mademoiselle.

             Dinah M. Muloch Craik.

ÉTUDE RÉALISTE.

I.

A BABY's feet, like sea-shells pink,
   Might tempt, should heaven see meet,
An angel's lips to kiss, we think,
   A baby's feet

Like rose-hued sea-flowers toward the heat
   They stretch and spread and wink
Their ten soft buds that part and meet.

No flower-bells that expand and shrink
   Gleam half so heavenly sweet,
As shine on life's untrodden brink
   A baby's feet.

II.

A baby's hands, like rose-buds furled
    Where yet no leaf expands,
Ope if you touch, though close upcurled,
    A baby's hands.

Then, fast as warriors grip their brands
    When battle's bolt is hurled,
They close, clenched hard like tightening bands.

No rose-buds yet by dawn impearled
    Match, even in loveliest lands,
The sweetest flowers in all the world—
    A baby's hands.

III.

A baby's eyes, ere speech begin,
    Ere lips learn words or sighs,
Bless all things bright enough to win
    A baby's eyes.

Love, while the sweet thing laughs and lies,
    And sleep flows out and in,
Sees perfect in them Paradise !

Their glance might cast out pain and sin,
    Their speech make dumb the wise,
By mute glad godhead felt within
    A baby's eyes.

Algernon Charles Swinburne.

NOT A CHILD.

I.

"Not a child : I call myself a boy,"
Says my king, with accent stern yet mild,
Now nine years have brought him change of joy ;
  " Not a child."

How could reason be so far beguiled,
Err so far from sense's safe employ,
Stray so wide of truth, or run so wild ?

Seeing his face bent over book or toy,
Child I called him, smiling : but he smiled
Back, as one too high for vain annoy—
  Not a child.

II.

Not a child ! alack the year !
What should ail an undefiled
Heart, that he would fain appear
  Not a child ?

Man, with years of memories piled
Each on other, far and near,
Fain again would be so styled :

Fain would cast off hope and fear,
Rest, forget, be reconciled :
Why would you so fain be, dear,
  Not a child ?

III.

Child or boy, my darling, which you will,
Still your praise finds heart and song employ,
Heart and song both yearning toward you still,
    Child or boy.

All joys else might sooner pall or cloy
Love than this which inly takes its fill,
Dear, of sight of your more perfect joy.

Nay, be aught you please, let all fulfil
All your pleasure ; be your world your toy:
Mild or wild we love you, loud or still,
    Child or boy.
            Algernon Charles Swinburne.

A CHILD'S PITY.

No sweeter thing than children's ways and wiles,
    Surely, we say, can gladden eyes and ears ;
Yet sometimes sweeter than their words or smiles
    Are even their tears.

To one for once a piteous tale was read,
    How, when the murderous mother crocodile
Was slain, her fierce brood famished, and lay dead,
    Starved, by the Nile.

In vast green reed-beds on the vast grey slime
    These monsters motionless and helpless lay,
Perishing only for the parent's crime
    Whose seed were they.

Hours after, toward the dusk, one blithe small bird
　Of Paradise, who has our hearts in keeping,
Was heard or seen, but hardly seen or heard,
　　For pity weeping.

He was so sorry, sitting still apart,
　For the poor little crocodiles, he said.
Six years had given him, for an angel's heart,
　　A child's instead.

Feigned tears the false beasts shed for murderous ends,
　We know from travellers' tales of crocodiles ;
But these tears wept upon them of my friend's
　　Outshine his smiles.

What heavenliest angels of what heavenly city
　Could match the heavenly heart in children here?
The heart that hallowing all things with its pity
　　Casts out all fear?

So lovely, so divine, so dear their laughter
　Seems to us, we know not what could be more dear:
But lovelier yet we see the sign thereafter
　　Of such a tear.

With sense of love half laughing and half weeping
　We met your tears, our small sweet-spirited friend :
Let your love have us in its heavenly keeping
　　To life's last end.

　　　　　　　Algernon Charles Swinburne.

OUR WHITE ROSE.

ALL in our marriage garden
　　Grew, smiling up to God,
A bonnier flower than ever
　　Suckt the green warmth of the sod.
O beautiful unfathomably
　　Its little life unfurled ;
Life's crowning sweetness was our wee
　　White Rose of all the world.

From out a gracious bosom,
　　Our bud of beauty grew ;
It fed on smiles for sunshine,
　　And tears for daintier dew.
Aye nestling warm and tenderly,
　　Our leaves of love were curled
So close and close about our wee
　　White Rose of all the world.

Two flowers of glorious crimson
　　Grew with our Rose of Light ;
Still kept the sweet heaven-grafted slip
　　Her whiteness saintly white.
In the winds of life they danced with glee,
　　And reddened as it whirled ;
White, white and wondrous grew our wee
　　White Rose of all the world.

With mystical faint fragrance
　　Our house of life she filled—
Revealed each hour some fairy tower,
　　Where wingèd hope might build.

We saw—though none like us might see—
   Such precious promise pearled
Upon the petals of our wee
   White Rose of all the world.

But evermore the halo
   Of angel-light increased ;
Like the mystery of moonlight,
   That folds some fairy feast.
Snow-white, snow-soft, snow-silently,
   Our darling bud up-curled,
And dropt in the Grave-God's lap—our wee
   White Rose of all the world.

Our Rose was but in blossom ;
   Our life was but in spring ;
When down the solemn midnight
   We heard the spirits sing :
" Another bud of infancy,
   With holy dews impearled ; "
And in their hands they bore our wee
   White Rose of all the world.

You scarce would think so small a thing
   Could leave a loss so large ;
Her little light such shadow fling,
   From dawn to sunset's marge.
In other springs our life may be
   In bannered bloom unfurled ;
But never, never match our wee
   White Rose of all the world.

                    Gerald Massey.

WITHIN A MILE.

WITHIN a mile of Edinburgh town
We laid our little darling down;
Our first seed in God's acre sown!

So sweet a place! Death looks beguiled
Of half his gloom; or sure he smiled
To win our lovely, spirit child.

God giveth his beloved sleep
So calm, within its silence deep,
As angel-guards its watch did keep.

The City looketh solemn and sweet;
It bares a gentle brow, to greet
The mourners mourning at its feet.

The sea of human life breaks round
This shore o' the dead, with softened sound:
Wild flowers climb each mossy mound

To place in resting hands their palm,
And breathe their beauty, bloom and balm;
Folding the dead in fragrant calm.

A softer shadow Grief might wear;
And old Heartache come gather there
The peace that falleth after prayer.

Poor heart, that danced along the vines
All reeling-ripe with wild love-wines,
Thou walk'st with Death among the pines!

Lorn Mother, at the dark grave-door,
She kneeleth, pleading o'er and o'er ;
But it is shut for evermore.

She toileth on, the mournfull'st thing,
At the vain task of emptying
The cistern whence the salt tears spring.

Blind ! blind ! she feels, but cannot read
Aright ; then leans as she would feed
The dear dead lips that never heed.

The spirit of life may leap above,
But in that grave her prisoned dove
Lies, cold to the warm embrace of love,

And dark, tho' all the world be bright ;
And lonely, with a City in sight ;
And desolate in the rainy night.

Ah, God ! when in the glad life-cup
The face of Death swims darkly up ;
The crowning flower is sure to droop.

And so we laid our darling down,
When summer's cheek grew ripely brown,
And still, tho' grief hath milder grown,

Unto the Stranger's land we cleave,
Like some poor Birds that grieve and grieve,
Round the robbed nest, and cannot leave.

Gerald Massey.

TO A VERY YOUNG LADY.

O GAY little girl with the merry brown eyes
  Looking over my sheet as I scribble this twaddle,
Suppose I attempt just to make a surmise
  In regard to the thoughts of your giddy young noddle.

Theology—politics—science? Pooh, pooh!
  Learn *them* for some twenty years after your bridal.
Young ladies of eight are a bore if they're blue:
  " The Whole Duty of Girls " to be happy and idle.

You don't care a pin about Louis the Knave,
  What schemes he is planning, what quarrel he'll fish
    up :
You care just as little though John Bright may rave,
  Or Palmerston make an unorthodox Bishop.

To you a ridiculous sight it would seem
  If Tory and Radical came to a tussle :
You approve of ripe strawberries smothered in cream,
  But not of Reform and its hero, John Russell.

    .   .   .   .   .   .

What cares my young heroine, singing her tune,
  And considering Wednesday a thoroughly jolly day,
For June has consented at last to be June,
  With blue sky and dry grass and Papa making holiday.

                          Mortimer Collins.

THE LULLABY.

I SAW two children hushed to death,
   In lap of One with silver wings,
Holding a lute, whose latest breath
   Still lingered on the trembling strings.

Her face was very pale and fair,
   And from her hooded eyes was shed
A love celestial, and her hair
   Was like a crown around her head.

The smallest wave will she displace
   That fills the lute's faint-ebbing strain ;
The notes seem echoed from her face,
   And echoed back from theirs again.

               William Allingham.

HALF-WAKING.

I THOUGHT it was the little bed
   I slept in long ago ;
A straight white curtain at the head,
   And two smooth knobs below.

I thought I saw the nursery fire,
   And in a chair well-known
My mother sat, and did not tire
   With reading all alone.

If I should make the slightest sound
    To show that I'm awake,
She'd rise, and lap the blankets round,
    My pillow softly shake ;

Kiss me, and turn my face to see
    The shadows on the wall,
And then sing *Rousseau's Dream* to me,
    Till fast asleep I fall.

But this is not my little bed ;
    That time is far away ;
'Mong strangers cold I live instead,
    From dreary day to day.

               William Allingham.

THE BEDOUIN CHILD.

[Among the Bedouins, a father, in enumerating his children, never counts his daughters, for a daughter is considered a disgrace.]

ILYAS the prophet, lingering near the moon,
    Heard from a tent a child's heart-withering wail,
    Mixt with the sorrow of the nightingale,
And, entering, found, sunk in mysterious swoon,
A little maiden dreaming there alone :—
    She babbled of her father sitting pale
    'Neath wings of Death—'mid sights of sorrow and
        bale—
And pleaded for his life in piteous tone.

" Poor child, plead on," the succouring prophet saith,
  While she, with eager lips, like one who tries
  To kiss a dream, stretches her arms and cries
To Heaven for help—" Plead on ; such pure love-
    breath,
Reaching the Throne, might stay the wings of Death
  That, in the Desert, fan thy father's eyes."

The drouth-slain camels lie on every hand ;
  Seven sons await the morning vultures' claws ;
  'Mid empty water-skins and camel-maws
The father sits, the last of all the band.
He mutters, drowsing o'er the moonlit sand,
  " Sleep fans my brow: 'Sleep makes us all pashas;'
  Or, if the wings are Death's, why Azraeel draws
A childless father from an empty land."

"Nay," saith a voice, "the wind of Azraeel's wings
  A child's sweet breath hath stilled; so God decrees:"
  A camel's bell comes tinkling on the breeze,
Filling the Bedouin's brain with bubble of springs
  And scent of flowers and shadow of wavering trees,
Where, from a tent, a little maiden sings.

                                    Theodore Watts.

A GIPSY-CHILD'S CHRISTMAS.

DEAR Sinfi rose and danced along " The Dells,"
  Drawn by the Christmas chimes, and soon she sate
  Where 'neath the snow around the churchyard gate
The ploughmen slept in bramble-banded cells.

The gorgios passed, half fearing gipsy spells,
  While Sinfi, gazing, seemed to meditate;
  She laughed for joy, then wept disconsolate:
"De poor dead gorgios cannot hear de bells."

Within the church the clouds of gorgio-breath
  Arose to One in lazy praise and prayer.
  But where stood He? Beside our Sinfi there,
Remembering childish tears in Nazareth,
  Building of love the golden Christmas-stair
O'er sorrow and sin and wintry deeps of Death.
                  Theodore Watts.

MARTIN'S PUZZLE.

THERE she goes up the street, with her book in her hand,
  And her Good morning, Martin! Ay, lass, how d'ye
    do?
Very well, thank you, Martin! I can't understand!
  I might just as well never have cobbled a shoe!
I can't understand it. She talks like a song;
  Her voice takes your ear like the ring of a glass;
She seems to give gladness while limping along,
  Yet sinner ne'er suffer'd like that little lass.

First, a fool of a boy ran her down with a cart.
  Then, her fool of a father—a blacksmith by trade—
Why the deuce does he tell us it half broke his heart?
  His heart!—where's the leg of the poor little maid?
Well, that's not enough; they must push her down-
    stairs,
  To make her go crooked; but why count the list?
If it's right to suppose that our human affairs
  Are all order'd by heaven—there, bang goes my fist!

For if angels can look on such sights—never mind !
　When you're next to blaspheming, it's best to be
　　mum.
The parson declares that her woes weren't designed ;
　But then, with the parson it's all kingdom-come.
Lose a leg, save a soul—a convenient text ;
　I call it tea doctrine, not savouring of God.
When poor little Molly wants chastening, why, next
　The Archangel Michael might taste of the rod.

But, to see the poor darling go limping for miles
　To read books to sick people !—and just of an age
When girls learn the meaning of ribands and smiles !
　Makes me feel like a squirrel that turns in a cage.
The more I push thinking, the more I revolve :
　I never get farther ;—and as to her face,
It starts up when near on my puzzle I solve,
　And says, "This crush'd body seems such a sad
　　case."

Not that she's for complaining ; she reads to earn pence ;
　And from those who can't pay, simple thanks are
　　enough.
Does she leave lamentation for chaps without sense ?
　Howsoever, she's made up of wonderful stuff.
Ay, the soul in her body must be a stout cord ;
　She sings little hymns at the close of the day,
Though she has but three fingers to lift to the Lord,
　And only one leg to kneel down with and pray.

What I ask is, why persecute such a poor dear,
　If there's Law above all ?　Answer that if you can !
Irreligious I'm not ; but I look on this sphere
　As a place where a man should just think like a man.

It isn't fair dealing ! But, contrariwise,
  Do bullets in battle the wicked select ?
Why, then it's all chance-work ! And yet, in her eyes,
  She holds a fixed something by which I am checked.

Yonder riband of sunshine aslope on the wall,
  If you eye it a minute 'll have the same look ;
So kind ! and so merciful ! God of us all !
  It's the very same lesson we get from the Book.
Then, is Life but a trial ? Is that what is meant ?
  Some must toil, and some perish, for others below :
The injustice to each spreads a common content ;
  Aye ! I've lost it again, for it can't be quite so.

She's the victim of fools : that seems near the mark.
  On earth there are engines and numerous fools.
Why the Lord can permit them, we're still in the
    dark ;
  He does, and in some sort of way they're His tools.
It's a roundabout way, with respect let me add,
  If Molly goes crippled that we may be taught ;
But, perhaps it's the only way, though it's so bad ;
  In that case we'll bow down our heads,—as we ought.

But the worst of *me* is, that when I bow my head,
  I perceive a thought wriggling away in the dust,
And I follow its tracks, quite forgetful, instead
  Of humble acceptance : for, question I must !
Here's a creature made carefully—carefully made !
  Put together with craft, and then stamped on, and
    why?
The answer seems nowhere : it's discord that's played.
  The sky's a blue dish ! an implacable sky !

34

Stop a moment.   I seize an idea from the pit.
   They tell us that discord, though discord, alone,
Can be harmony when the notes properly fit :
   Am I judging all things from a single false tone?
Is the Universe one immense organ, that rolls
   From devils to angels?   I'm blind with the sight.
It pours such a splendour on heaps of poor souls !
   I might try at kneeling with Molly to-night.

George Meredith.

THE YOUNG USURPER.

On my darling's bosom
Has dropped a living rosebud,
   Fair as brilliant Hesper
Against the brimming flood.
      She handles him,
      She dandles him,
   She fondles him and eyes him :
And if upon a tear he wakes,
   With many a kiss she dries him :
She covets every move he makes,
   And never enough can prize him.
      Ah, the young Usurper !
      I yield my golden throne :
      Such angel bands attend his hands
      To claim it for his own.

George Meredith.

JOHNNY.

*(Founded on an Anecdote on the First French
Revolution.)*

JOHNNY had a golden head
  Like a golden mop in blow,
Right and left his curls would spread
  In a glory and a glow,
And they framed his honest face
Like stray sunbeams out of place.

Long and thick, they half could hide
  How threadbare his patched jacket hung;
They used to be his mother's pride;
  She praised them with a tender tongue,
And stroked them with a loving finger,
That smoothed and stroked and loved to
    linger.

On a doorstep Johnny sat,
  Up and down the street looked he;
Johnny did not own a hat,
  Hot or cold tho' days might be;
Johnny did not own a boot
To cover up his muddy foot.

Johnny's face was pale and thin,
  Pale with hunger and with crying;
For his mother lay within,
  Talked and tossed and seemed a-dying,
While Johnny racked his brain to think
How to get her help and drink,

Get her physic, get her tea,
　Get her bread and something nice ;
Not a penny-piece had he ;
　And scarce a shilling might suffice ;
No wonder that his soul was sad,
When not one penny-piece he had.

As he sat there, thinking, moping,
　Because his mother's wants were many,
Wishing much, but scarcely hoping
　To earn a shilling or a penny,
A friendly neighbour passed him by
And questioned him—Why did he cry ?

Alas ! his trouble soon was told :
　He did not cry for cold or hunger,
Though he was hungry both and cold ;
　He only felt more weak and younger,
Because he wished so to be old
And apt at earning pence or gold.

Kindly that neighbour was, but poor,
　Scant coin had he to give or lend ;
And well he guessed those needed more
　Than pence or shillings to befriend
The helpless woman in her strait,
So much loved, yet so desolate.

One way he saw, and only one :
　He would—he could not—give the advice,
And yet he must : the widow's son
　Had curls of gold would fetch their price ;
Long curls which might be clipped, and sold
For silver, or perhaps for gold.

Our Johnny, when he understood
  Which shop it was that purchased hair,
Ran off as briskly as he could,
  And in a trice stood cropped and bare,
Too short of hair to fill a locket,
But jingling money in his pocket.

Precious money, tea and bread,
  Physic, ease, for mother dear,
Better than a golden head :
  Yet our hero dropped a tear
When he spied himself close-shorn,
Barer much than lamb new-born.

His mother throve upon the money,
  Ate and revived, and kissed her son :
But oh ! when she perceived her Johnny,
  And understood what he had done,
All and only for her sake,
She sobbed as if her heart would break.
                    Christina Rossetti.

BUDS AND BABIES.

A MILLION buds are born that never blow,
  That sweet with promise lift a pretty head,
To blush and wither on a barren bed,
  And leave no fruit to show.

Sweet, unfulfilled.   Yet have I understood
  One joy, by their fragility made plain :
Nothing was ever beautiful in vain,
  Or all in vain was good.
                    Christina Rossetti.

THE SNOWDROP MONUMENT.

(*In Lichfield Cathedral.*)

MARVELS of sleep grown cold !
    Who hath not longed to fold
With pitying ruth, forgetful of their bliss,
    Those cherub forms that lie,
    With none to watch them nigh,
Or touch the silent lips with one warm human kiss ?

    What ! they are left alone
    All night with graven stone,
Pillars and arches that above them meet ;
    While through those windows high
    The journeying stars can spy,
And dim blue moonbeams drop on their uncovered feet !

    O cold ! yet look again,
    There is a wandering vein
Traced in the hand where those white snowdrops lie.
    Let her rapt dreamy smile
    The wandering heart beguile,
That almost thinks to hear a calm contented sigh

    What silence dwells between
    Those severed lips serene !
The rapture of sweet waiting breathes and grows ;
    What trance-like peace is shed
    On her reclining head,
And e'en on listless feet what languor of repose !

    Angels of joy and love
    Lean softly from above
And whisper to her sweet and marvellous things ;

Tell of the golden gate
That opened wide doth wait,
And shadow her dim sleep with their celestial wings.

Hearing of that blest shore
She thinks of earth no more,
Contented to forego this wintry land.
She hath nor thought or care
But to rest calmly there,
And hold the snowdrops pale that blossoms in her
hand.

But on the other face
Broodeth a mournful grace,
This had foreboding thoughts beyond her years;
While sinking thus to sleep
She saw her mother weep,
And could not lift her hand to dry those heart-sick
tears.

Could not—but failing lay,
Sighed her young life away,
And let her arm drop down in listless rest,
Too weary on that bed
To turn her dying head,
Or fold the little sister nearer to her breast.

Yet this is faintly told
On features fair and cold,
A look of calm surprise, of mild regret,
As if with life oppressed
She turned her to her rest,
But felt her mother's love and looked not to forget.

How wistfully they close,
Sweet eyes, to their repose !
How quietly declines the placid brow !
The young lips seem to say,
" I have wept much to-day,
And felt some bitter pains, but they are over now."

Sleep ! there are left below
Many who pine to go,
Many who lay it to their chastened souls,
That gloomy days draw nigh,
And they are blest who die,
For this green world grows worse the longer that
she rolls.

And as for me, I know
A little of her woe,
Her yearning want doth in my soul abide,
And sighs of them that weep,
" O put us soon to sleep,
For when we wake—with Thee—we shall be
satisfied."

Jean Ingelow.

LITTLE ELLA.

I KNOW not, little Ella, what the flowers
Said to you then, to make your cheek so pale ;
And why the blackbird in our laurel bowers
Spoke to you, only : and the poor pink snail
Fear'd less your steps than those of the May-shower.
It was not strange those creatures loved you so,
And told you all.   'Twas not so long ago
You were, yourself, a bird, or else a flower.

And, little Ella, you were pale, because
   So soon you were to die.   I know that now,—
And why there even seem'd a sort of gauze
   Over your deep blue eyes, and sad young brow.
You were too good to grow up, Ella, you,
   And be a woman such as I have known !
   And so upon your heart they put a stone,
And left you, dear, amongst the flowers and dew.

O thou, the morning star of my dim soul !
   My little elfin-friend from Fairy-Land !
Whose memory is yet innocent of the whole
   Of that which makes me doubly need thy hand,
Thy guiding hand from mine so soon withdrawn !
   Here where I find so little like to thee :
   For thou wert as the breath of dawn to me,
Starry, and pure, and brief as is the dawn.

Thy knight was I, and thou my Fairy Queen,
   ('Twas in the days of love and chivalry !)
And thou dids't hide thee in a bower of green.
   But thou so well hast hidden thee, that I
Have never found thee since.   And thou didst set
   Many a task, and quest, and high emprize,
   Ere I should win my guerdon from thine eyes,
So many, and so many, that not yet

My tasks are ended, nor my wanderings o'er.
   But some day there will come across the main
A magic barque, and I shall quit this shore
   Of care, and find thee in thy bower again ;
And thou wilt say, " My brother, hast thou found
   Our home at last ?" . . . Whilst I, in answer, Sweet,
   Shall heap my life's last booty at thy feet,
And bare my breast with many a bleeding wound.

The spoils of time ! the trophies of the world !
  The keys of conquered towns, and captived kings,
And many a broken sword, and banner furl'd,
  The heads of giants, and swart soldan's rings,
And many a maiden's scarf, and many a wand
    Of baffled wizard, many an amulet,
    And many a shield with mine own heart's blood wet,
And jewels rare from many a distant land !

How sweet, with thee, my sister, to renew,
  In lands of light, the search for those bright birds
Of plumage so ethereal in its hue,
  And music sweeter than all mortal words,
Which some good angel to our childhood sent
    With messenger from Paradisal flowers,
    So lately left, the scent of Eden bowers
Yet linger'd in our hair, where'er we went !

Now, they are all fled by, this many a year,
  Adown the viewless valleys of the wind,
And never more will cross this hemisphere,
    Those birds of passage !   Never shall I find,
Dropt from the flight you follow'd, dear, so far
    That you will never come again, I know,
    One plumelet on the paths whereby I go,
Throwing thy light there, O my morning star !

She pass'd out of my youth, at the still time
  O' the early light, when all was green and husht.
She pass'd, and pass'd away.   Some broken rhyme
  Scrawl'd on the panel or the pane : the crusht
And faded rose she dropp'd ; the page she turn'd
    And finish'd not ; the ribbon on the knot   [not !
    That flutter'd from her . . . Stranger, harm them
I keep these sacred relics undiscern'd.

                    Lord Lytton (*" Owen Meredith "*).

BABY BELL.

I.

HAVE you not heard the poets tell
How came the dainty Baby Bell
   Into this world of woe?
The gates of Heaven were left ajar :
   With folded hands and dreamy eyes,
   Wandering out of Paradise,
She saw this planet like a star,
   Hung in the depth of even—
Its bridges, running to and fro,
O'er which the white-winged Angels go,
   Bearing the holy Dead to Heaven !
   She touched a bridge of flowers—her feet,
So light they did not bend the bells
Of the celestial asphodels !
They fell like dew upon the flowers,
   And all the air grew strangly sweet !
And thus came dainty Baby Bell
   Into this world of ours.

II.

She came and brought delicious May.
   The swallows built beneath the eaves ;
   Like sunlight in and out the leaves,
The robin went, the livelong day ;
The lily swung its noiseless bell,
   And o'er the porch the trembling vine
   Seemed bursting with its veins of wine.
How sweetly, softly twilight fell !
O, earth was full of singing birds,
   And happy spring-tide flowers,
When the dainty Baby Bell
   Came to this world of ours.

III.

O Baby, dainty Baby Bell,
How fair she grew from day to day !
  What woman-nature filled her eyes,
What poetry within them lay !
Those deep and tender twilight eyes,
  So full of meaning, pure and bright,
  As if she yet stood in the light
Of those oped gates of Paradise !
  And we loved Baby more and more:
  Ah, never in our hearts before
    Was love so lovely born:
  We felt we had a link between
  This real world and that unseen—
    The land beyond the morn !
And for the love of those dear eyes,
  For love of her whom God led forth
  (The mother's being ceased on earth
When Baby come from Paradise),
For love of Him who smote our lives,
  And woke the chords of joy and pain,
We said, " Sweet Christ ! "—our hearts bent down
  Like violets after rain.

IV.

And now the orchards, which in June
  Were white and rosy in their bloom—
Filling the crystal veins of air
  With gentle pulses of perfume—
Were rich in Autumn's mellow prime :
The plums were globes of honeyed wine,
The hivèd sweets of summer time !

The ivory chestnut burst its shell :
The soft-cheeked peaches blushed and fell !
The grapes were purpling in the grange,
And time brought just as rich a change
   In little Baby Bell.
Her tiny form more perfect grew,
   And in her features we could trace,
   In softened curves, her mother's face !
Her angel-nature ripened too.
We thought her lovely when she came,
   But she was holy, saintly now . . . .
   Around her pale angelic brow
We saw a slender ring of flame !

V.

God's hand had taken away the seal
   Which held the portals of her speech ;
And oft she said a few strange words
   Whose meaning lay beyond our reach.
She never was a child to us,
   We never held her being's key :
We could not teach her holy things ;
   She was Christ's self in purity !

VI.

It came upon us by degrees :
   We saw its shadow ere it fell,
The knowledge that our God had sent
   His messenger for Baby Bell.
We shuddered with unlanguaged pain,
   And all our hopes were changed to fears,
   And all our thoughts ran into tears
Like sunshine into rain.

We cried aloud in our behalf,
 " O, smite us gently, gently God !
Teach us to bend and kiss the rod,
 And perfect grow through grief ! "
Ah, how we loved her, God can tell ;
Her little heart was cased in ours :
 Our hearts are broken, Baby Bell !

VII.

At last he came, the messenger,
 The messenger from unseen lands :
And what did dainty Baby Bell ?
 She only crossed her little hands,
She only looked more meek and fair !
We parted back her silken hair ;
We laid some buds upon her brow,
White buds like summer's drifted snow—
 Death's bride arrayed in flowers !
And thus went dainty Baby Bell,
 Out of this world of ours !
                  · *Thomas Bailey Aldrich.*

A BIRTH SONG.

I.

THE red cock waked ere day was born,
And feasted full on barley corn ;
And then he vaulted on the wall,
 And blew a blast upon his horn,
As if to say, " Take notice all,
 I am the finest bird of morn ! "
Proud fool ! So dingy red and yellow ;
The blackbird was a prettier fellow.

The blackbird from an alder nigh,
Unlocked his golden-lidded eye,
And scanned the silent silvering east :
  Then dropped into the cool green rye,
And made the early worm his feast ;
  Then sang he to the morning sky—
Defiant—yet O clear and sweet,
As if no lark was at his feet.

The lark—the bird that sleeps in dew,
And sings in heaven so dim and blue—
Ashamed that he had dreamed so long,
  With speed despatched a grub or two,
Then rose on wing supreme and strong,
  And sang his song divine and true :
Long, emulous, on the notes he hung,
As if there was no human tongue.

But on that budding April morn,
A tender human babe was born,
Whose eyelids trembled in the dawn
  Like two white lily-buds forlorn ;
Whose faint cries wavered o'er the lawn,
  And seemed to fill the birds with scorn :
But soon they ceased, abashed and dumb—
The voice and soul of life had come !

II.

Let birds and waters warble clear ;
  More sweet this infant voice to me,
Which comes as from the golden sphere,
  Where thrills the soul of harmony—
No myriad-mouthéd organ can
  Out-melody God-moulded man.

Let sceptres flash, and senates shake ;
  The war-steed neigh, the trumpet blow ;
Let banners strike the wind, and make
  A splendour where the warriors go—
Within this new-born maiden's eyes
The glory of all conquest lies.

Let knowledge, glimmering on the brine,
  Bind isle to isle, and clime to clime,
And through the deep sea's lyric line
  Twangle the piercing psalms of time,
This baby-maid's untunéd soul
Shall yet a grander psalm outroll.

For in her soul, serene and clear,
  All mortal and immortal shine ;
Eternity, a single year,
  Thought glowing into light divine:
The sweetness of the years to be
Is hers, God-given virginity.

III.

All night the moon was listening
  To the nightingale ;
And the glow-worm was glistening
  In the grass-green vale.

All night the ships were dancing,
  Through the far foam hurled ;
All night the dawn was glancing
  From the underworld.

All night the stars were creeping
  Towards the ocean swell ;
All night the rose was weeping
  O'er the mossy well.

All night, through realms Elysian,
　Mother wandered far,
And claspt in arms of vision
　Baby like a star.
　　　　　　William Freeland.

DICKENS IN CAMP.

Above the pines the moon was slowly dimpling,
　　The river sang below ;
The dim Sierras, from beyond, uplifting
　　Their minarets of snow.

The roaring camp-fire, with rude humour, painted
　　The ruddy tints of health
On haggard face and form that drooped and fainted
　　In the fierce race for wealth ;

Till one arose, and from his pack's scant treasure
　　A hoarded volume drew,
And cards were dropped from hands of listless leisure
　　To hear the tale anew ;

And then, while round them shadows gathered faster,
　　And as the fire-light fell,
He read aloud the book wherein the Master
　　Had writ of " Little Nell."

Perhaps 'twas boyish fancy—for the reader
　　Was youngest of them all—
But, as he read, from clustering pine and cedar
　　A silence seemed to fall ;

35

The fir-trees, gathering closer in the shadows,
    Listened in every spray,
While the whole camp, with "Nell" on English
    meadows,
    Wandered and lost their way.

And so in mountain solitudes—o'ertaken
    As by some spell divine—
Their cares dropped from them like the needles shaken
    From out the gusty pine.

Lost is that camp, and wasted all its fire :
    And he who wrought that spell ?—
Ah, towering pine and stately Kentish spire,
    Ye have one tale to tell !

Lost is that camp ! but let its fragrant story
    Blend with the breath that thrills
With hop-vines' incense all the Persian glory
    That fills the Kentish hills.

And on that grave where English oak and holly
    And laurel wreaths entwine,
Deem it not all a too presumptuous folly,—
    This spray of Western pine !

                              Bret Harte.

DAISY'S VALENTINES.

ALL night, through Daisy's sleep, it seems,
    Have ceaseless " rat-tats " thundered ;
All night through Daisy's rosy dreams
    Have devious Postmen blundered,

Delivering letters round her bed,—
Suggestive missives, sealed with red,
And franked, of course, with due Queen's-head—
    While Daisy lay and wondered.

But now, when chirping birds begin,
    And Day puts off the Quaker,—
When Cook renews her morning din,
    And rates the cheerful baker,—
She dreams her dream no dream at all,
For, just as pigeons come to call,
Winged letters flutter down, and fall
    Around her head, and wake her.

Yes, there they are ! With quirk and twist,
    And fraudful arts directed ;
(Save Grandpapa's dear stiff old " fist,"
    Through all disguise detected ;)
But which is his,—her young Lothair's—
Who wooed her on the schoolroom stairs
With three sweet cakes, and two ripe pears,
    In one neat pile collected ?

'Tis there, be sure. Though, truth to speak
    (If truth may be permitted),
I doubt that young " gift-bearing Greek "
    Is scarce for fealty fitted :
For has he not (I grieve to say),
To two loves more, on this same day,
In just this same emblazoned way,
    His transient vows transmitted?

He may be true. Yet, Daisy dear,
    That even youth grows colder
You'll find is no new thing, I fear ;
    And when you're somewhat older

You'll read of one Dardanian boy
Who "wooed with gifts" a maiden coy—
Then took the morning train to Troy,
    In spite of all he'd told her.

But wait. Your time will come. And then,
    Obliging Fates, please send her
The nicest thing you have in men,
    Sound-hearted, strong, and tender ;—
The kind of man, dear Fates, you know,
That feels how shyly Daisies grow,
And what soft things they are, and so
    Will spare to spoil or mend her.

                    Austin Dobson.

THE CRADLE.

How steadfastly she'd worked at it !
    How lovingly had drest,
With all her would-be-mother's wit,
    That little rosy nest !

How lovingly she'd hang on it !—
    It sometimes seemed, she said,
There lay beneath its coverlet
    A little sleeping head.

He came at last, the tiny guest,
    Ere bleak December fled ;
That rosy nest he never prest—
    Her coffin was its bed.

                    Austin Dobson.

THE DEAD MOTHER.

I.

As I lay asleep, as I lay asleep,
Under the grass as I lay so deep,
As I lay asleep in my white death-serk
Under the shade of Our Lady's Kirk,
I waken'd up in the dead of night,
I waken'd up in my shroud o' white,
And I heard a cry from far away,
And I knew the voice of my daughter May:
" Mother, mother, come hither to me !
Mother, mother, come hither and see !
Mother, mother, mother dear,
Another mother is sitting here :
My body is bruised, in pain I cry,
All night long on the straw I lie,
I thirst and hunger for drink and meat,
And mother, mother, to sleep were sweet !"
I heard the cry, though my grave was deep,
And awoke from sleep, and awoke from sleep.

II.

I awoke from sleep, I awoke from sleep,
Up I rose from my grave so deep !
The earth was black, but overhead
The stars were yellow, the moon was red ;
And I walk'd along all white and thin,
And lifted the latch and enter'd in.
I reach'd the chamber as dark as night,
And though it was dark my face was white :
" Mother, mother, I look on thee !
Mother, mother, you frighten me !

For your cheeks are thin and your hair is grey!"
But I smiled, and kissed her tears away;
I smooth'd her hair and I sang a song,
And on my knee I rock'd her long.
"O mother, mother, sing low to me—
I am sleepy now, and I cannot see!"
I kiss'd her, but I could not weep,
And she went to sleep, she went to sleep.

III.

As we lay asleep, as we lay asleep,
My May and I, in our grave so deep,
As we lay asleep in the midnight mirk,
Under the shade of Our Lady's Kirk,
I waken'd up in the dead of night,
Though May my daughter lay warm and white,
And I heard the cry of a little one,
And I knew 'twas the voice of Hugh, my son:
"Mother, mother, come hither to me!
Mother, mother, come hither and see!
Mother, mother, mother dear,
Another mother is sitting here:
My body is bruised and my heart is sad,
But I speak my mind and call them bad;
I thirst and hunger night and day,
And were I strong I would fly away!"
I heard the cry, though my grave was deep,
And awoke from sleep, and awoke from sleep!

IV.

I awoke from sleep, I awoke from sleep,
Up I rose from my grave so deep,
The earth was black, but overhead
The stars were yellow, the moon was red;

And I walk'd along all white and thin,
And lifted the latch and enter'd in.
" Mother, mother, and art thou here ?
I know your face, and I feel no fear ;
Raise me, mother, and kiss my cheek,
For oh, I am weary and sore and weak."
I smooth'd his hair with a mother's joy,
And he laugh'd aloud, my own brave boy ;
I raised and held him on my breast,
Sang him a song, and bade him rest.
" Mother, mother, sing low to me—
I am sleepy now, and I cannot see ! "
I kiss'd him, but I could not weep,
As he went to sleep, as he went to sleep.

v.

As I lay asleep, as I lay asleep,
With my girl and boy in my grave so deep,
As I lay asleep, I awoke in fear,
Awoke, but awoke not my children dear,
And heard a cry so low and weak
From a tiny voice that could not speak :
I heard the cry of a little one,
My bairn that could neither talk nor run,
My little, little one, uncaress'd,
Starving for lack of milk of the breast ;
And I rose from sleep and enter'd in,
And found my little one pinch'd and thin,
And croon'd a song, and hush'd its moan,
And put its lips to my white breast bone ;
And the red, red moon that lit the place
Went white to look at the little face,
And I kiss'd, and kiss'd, but could not weep,
As it went to sleep, as it went to sleep.

VI.

As it lay asleep, as it lay asleep,
I set it down in the darkness deep,
Smooth'd its limbs and laid it out,
And drew the curtains round about ;
Then into the dark, dark room I hied,
Where awake *he* lay, at the woman's side ;
And though the chamber was black as night,
He saw my face, for it was so white !
I gazed in his eyes, and he shriek'd in pain,
And I knew he would never sleep again,
And back to my grave crept silently,
And soon my baby was brought to me ;
My son and daughter beside me rest,
My little baby is on my breast,
Our bed is warm, and our grave is deep,
But he cannot sleep, he cannot sleep.

Robert Buchanan.

THE KING OF THE CRADLE.

DRAW back the cradle curtains, Kate,
    While watch and ward you're keeping,
Let's see the monarch in his state,
    And view him while he's sleeping.
He smiles and clasps his tiny hand,
    With sunbeams o'er him gleaming,—
A world of baby fairyland
    He visits while he's dreaming.

Monarch of pearly powder-puff,
　Asleep in nest so cosy,
Shielded from breath of breezes rough
　By curtains warm and rosy :
He slumbers soundly in his cell,
　As weak as one decrepid,
Though King of Coral, Lord of Bell,
　And Knight of Bath that's tepid.

Ah, lucky tyrant ! Happy lot !
　Fair watchers without number,
Who sweetly sing beside his cot,
　And hush him off to slumber ;
White hands in wait to smooth so neat
　His pillow when its rumpled—
A couch of rose leaves soft and sweet,
　Not one of which is crumpled !

Will yonder dainty dimpled hand—
　Size, nothing and a quarter—
E'er grasp a sabre, lead a band,
　To glory and to slaughter ?
Or, may I ask, will those blue eyes—
　In baby patois, " peepers "—
E'er in the House of Commons rise,
　And try to catch the Speaker's ?

Will that smooth brow o'er Hansard frown,
　Confused by lore statistic ?
Or will those lips e'er stir the town
　From pulpit ritualistic ?
Will e'er that tiny Sybarite
　Become an author noted ?
That little brain the world's delight,
　Its works by all men quoted ?

Though rosy, dimpled, plump, and round,
  Though fragile, soft, and tender,
Sometimes, alas ! it may be found
  The thread of life is slender !
A little shoe, a little glove—
  Affection never waning—
The shattered idol of our love
  Is all that is remaining!

Then does one chance, in fancy, hear,
  Small feet in childish patter,
Tread soft as they a grave draw near,
  And voices hush their chatter ;
'Tis small and new ; they pause in fear,
  Beneath the grey church tower,
To consecrate it with a tear,
  And deck it with a flower.

Who can predict the future, Kate—
  Your fondest aspiration !
Who knows the solemn laws of fate,
  That govern creation?
Who knows what lot awaits your boy—
  Of happiness or sorrow?
Sufficient for to-day is joy,
  Leave tears, Sweet, for to-morrow !

                    J. Ashby-Sterry.

THE TOY CROSS.

My little boy at Christmas-tide
  Made me a toy cross ;
Two sticks he did, in boyish pride,
  With brazen nail emboss.

Ah me ! how soon, on either side
   His dying bed's true cross,
She and I were crucified,
   Bemoaning our life-loss !

But He, whose arms in death spread wide
   Upon the holy tree,
Were clasped about him when he died—
   Clasped for eternity !

                  Hon. Roden Noel.

LAST VICTIMS FROM THE WRECK OF THE "PRINCESS ALICE."

I.

Two little bodies, from the tide
   Last gathered, lie alone ;
No father maddens by the side
   Of Love turned into stone ;
No mother weeps here for her pride,
   Her joy for ever flown.
They were all innocence and mirth,
   Warm light of loving eyes ;
They are defiled and ruined earth,
   The passing stranger flies.
The twain who watched them warmly curled,
   Asleep with locks of gold,
Felt that for them the whole wide world
   Nestled there aureoled.
And now they lie unknown, unnamed,
   In London's awful roar ;

Over them, piteous, unclaimed,
  Oblivion's dust will pour,
  Love's eyes look never more !
There is no silver sound, no speech,
  Although they rest so nigh,
No rosy, dimpled hands impleach
  In slumber tranquilly :
From the close clasp of loving arms,
  From heedless holiday,
Hurled upon death's dire alarms,
  And to uncared-for clay !

II.

Are they indeed unknown, unnamed ?
  Is any life spilt water ?
In the lone universe unclaimed !
  Souls for mad Chance to slaughter !
Have they no mother, and no father ?
  In all the world no friend ?
Are they a dim grey dust ? . . . nay rather
  Did their Eternal Parent send
Fair shining cohorts of His grace,
  Strong children of His love,
Who minister before His face,
  Swift-thronging from above,
To gather them from forth the gloom,
  Long ere men found their forms,
To shield them in the shock of doom,
  While heavenliest ardour warms
With emulation every breast ?
  All will be first to hold,
To lull the frightened babes to rest
  In their maternal fold !

There leaned both sire and mother lost,
  Dawning on the dim gaze;
And many sealed in death's deep frost,
  Fathers of former days,
Thronged all the approaches of God's throne,
  Whilst Christ arose above,
Smiling a welcome to His own
  Babe-brethren of His love.
. . . Yet ah ! the hideous prospect whirls !
  Death-slumber seems profound ;
With ghastly gleam the river swirls
  Blandly above the drowned !
. . . Nay, but the children are awake,
  Although we hear them not ;
Our dear ones their sweet prattle make
  In some fair, far cot.
I deem our life is a red flame
  Of purgatorial fire ;
And Death, God's calm white angel, came
  From the Eternal Sire,
To lay cool hands before their eyes,
  Shadowing from the glare,
And in profound tranquillities
  To hide from our despair.
One pure white Light is over all,
  One Spirit-Pulse serene ;
Who when we rise, and when we fall,
  Unmoved approves the scene.
For Love is Lord from Heaven to Hell,
  Walks our red waves of sorrow ;
Love weeps beside us ; all is well ;
  Day will dawn to-morrow.
Love weeps beside us, and within
  Love moaneth for our lot ;

Behold ! his vassals, Death and Sin,
   Chained to his chariot !
Love sleeps not, throned indifferent
   Upon a lordly scorn ;
He is the Man, whose brows are rent
   With sorrow's crown of thorn.
God is the God-forsaken Man ;
   He is the little child ;
His eyes with human woes are wan ;
   And all is reconciled.
                    Hon. Roden Noel.

ONLY A LITTLE CHILD.

A Voice.

ONLY a little child !
   Stone-cold upon a bed !
Is it for him you wail so wild,
   As though the very world were dead?
      Arise, arise !
Threaten not the tranquil skies !

Do not all things die ?
   'Tis but a faded flower !
Dear lives exhale perpetually
   With every fleeting hour.
Rachael for ever weeps her little ones ;
For ever Rizpah mourneth her slain sons.
      Arise, arise !
Threaten not the tranquil skies !

Only a little child !
   Long generations pass :

Behold them flash a moment wild
　With stormlight, a pale headlong mass
Of foam unto unfathomable gloom !
Worlds and shed leaves have all one doom.
　　　Arise, arise !
Threaten not the tranquil skies.

Should Earth's tremendous shade
　Spare only you and yours ?
Who regardeth empires fade
　Untroubled, who impassive pours
Human joy, a mere spilt water,
Revels red with human slaughter !
　　　Arise, arise !
Threaten not the tranquil skies.

Another Voice.

. . . Only a little child !
　He was the world to me.
Pierced to the heart, insane, defiled,
　All holiest hope ! foul mockery,
Childhood's innocent mirth and rest ;
Man's brief life a brutal jest.
　　　There is no God ;
Earth is Love's sepulchral sod !

Another Voice.

Only a little child !
　Ah ! then, who brought him here ?
Who made him loving, fair, and mild,
　And to your soul so dear ?
His lowly spirit seemed divine,
Burning in a heavenly shrine.
　　　Arise, arise !
With pardon for the tranquil skies.

Only a little child !
  Who sleeps upon God's heart !
Jesus blessed our undefiled,
  Whom no power avails to part
From the life of Him who died
And liveth, whatsoe'er betide !
      Whose are eyes
Tranquiller than starlit skies !

Only a little child !
  For whom all things are :
Spring and summer, winter wild,
  Sea and earth and every star,
Time, the void, pleasure and pain,
Hell and heaven, loss and gain !
Life and death, are his, and he
Rest's in God's eternity.
      Arise, arise !
Love is holy, true, and wise,
Mirrored in the tranquilled skies.

                      Hon. Roden Noel.

THE CHILDREN.

FATHER and mother, many a year
In rain and sunshine we have lived here,
    And the children—
And now that the winter days are come,
We wait and rest in own old home ;
    But where are the children?

All so young, in the times of old
Not a lamb was missing from our fold,
  And the children—
God's ways are narrow, the world is wide,
I would have guarded them at my side ;
  But where are the children?

We walk to the house of God alone,
From the last year's nest the birds have flown,
  And the children.—
Alone by the silent hearth we sit,
The chambers are ready, the fires are lit ;
  But where are the children?

My life is failing, my hair is grey,
I have seen the old years pass away,
  And the children—
My steps are feeble, my voice is low,
I am longing to bless you ere I go :
  But where are the children?

I had a dream of another home ;
I thought when He called us I should come,
  And the children—
And say, at the feet of Our Father in Heaven,
Here am I, with those Thou hast given :—
  But where are the children?

The day of the Lord is coming on ;
We shall meet again before God's throne,
  And the children—
Father and Mother, we trust, shall stand
Together then at God's right hand :—
  But where are the children?

      Mrs. Hamilton King.

A BOY'S ASPIRATIONS.

I WAS four yesterday : when I'm quite old,
I'll have a cricket ball made of pure gold ;
I'll carve the roast meat, and help soup and fish ;
I'll get my feet wet whenever I wish ;

I'll never go to bed till twelve o'clock ;
I'll make a mud pie in a clean frock ;
I'll whip naughty boys with a new birch ;
I'll take my guinea-pig always to church ;

I'll spend a hundred pounds every day ;
I'll have the alphabet quite done away ;
I'll have a parrot without a sharp beak ;
I'll see a pantomime six times a-week ;

I'll have a rose tree, always in bloom :
I'll keep a dancing bear in Mamma's room ;
I'll spoil my best clothes, and not care a pin ;
I'll have no visitors ever let in ;

I'll go at liberty upstairs or down ;
I'll pin a dishcloth to the cook's gown ;
I'll light the candles, and ring the big bell ;
I'll smoke Papa's pipe, feeling quite well ;

I'll have a ball of string, fifty miles long ;
I'll have a whistle as loud as the gong ;
I'll scold the housemaid for making a dirt ;
I'll cut my fingers without being hurt ;

I'll have my pinafores quite loose and nice ;
I'll wear great fishing-boots, like Captain Rice ;
I'll have a pot of beer at the girls' tea ;
I'll have John taught to say " Thank you " to me ;

I'll never stand up to show that I'm grown ;
No one shall say to me, " Don't throw a stone ! "
I'll drop my butter'd toast on the new chintz ;
I'll have no governess, giving her hints !

I'll have a nursery up in the stars ;
I'll lean through windows without any bars ;
I'll sail without my nurse in a big boat ;
I'll have no comforters tied round my throat ;

I'll have a language with not a word spell'd ;
I'll ride on horseback without being held ;
I'll hear Mamma say, " My boy, good as gold ! "
When I'm a grown-up man, sixty years old.

Menella Bute Smedley.

WOODEN LEGS.

Two children sat in the twilight,
   Murmuring soft and low :
Said one, " I'll be a sailor-lad,
   With my boat ahoy ! yo ho !
For sailors are most loved of all
   In every happy home,
And tears of grief or gladness fall
   Just as they go or come."

But the other child said sadly,
   " Ah, do not go to sea,
Or in the dreary winter nights
   What will become of me ?

For if the wind began to blow,
   Or thunder shook the sky,
Whilst you were in your boat, yo ho !
   What could I do but cry ? "

Then he said, "I'll be a soldier,
   With a delightful gun,
And I'll come home with a wooden leg,
   As heroes have often done."
She screams at that, and prays and begs,
   While tears—half anger—start,
"Don't talk about your wooden legs
   Unless you'd break my heart ! "

He answered her rather proudly,
   "If so, what can I be,
If I must not have a wooden leg,
   And must not go to sea ?
How could the Queen sleep sound at night,
   Safe from the scum and dregs,
If English boys refused to fight
   In fear of wooden legs ? "

She hung her head repenting,
   And trying to be good,
But her little hand stroked tenderly
   The leg of flesh and blood !
And with her rosy mouth she kiss'd
   The knickerbocker'd knee,
And sigh'd, "Perhaps—if you insist—
   You'd better go to sea ! "

Then he flung his arms about her,
   And laughingly he spoke,
"But I've seen many honest tars
   With legs of British oak !

Oh darling ! when I am a man,
　　With beard of shining black,
I'll be a *hero* if I can,
　　And you must not hold me back."

She kissed him as she answer'd,
　　" I'll try what I can do,—
And Wellington had both his legs,
　　And Cœur de Lion too !
And Garibaldi," here she sighed,
　　" I know *he's* lame—but there,
He's *such* a hero—none beside
　　Like *him* could do and dare ! "

So the children talk'd in the twilight
　　Of many a setting sun,
And she'd stroke his chin, and clap her hands,
　　That the beard had not begun ;
For though she meant to be brave and good,
　　When he played a hero's part,
Yet often the thought of the leg of wood
　　Hung heavy on her heart !

　　　　　　　　　　　　"*A.*"

───────

DEAF AND DUMB.

HE lies on the grass, looking up to the sky ;
Blue butterflies pass like a breath or a sigh,
The shy little hare runs confidingly near,
And wise rabbits stare with inquiry, not fear :
Gay squirrels have found him and made him their
　　choice ;
All creatures flock round him, and seem to rejoice.

Wild ladybirds leap on his cheek fresh and fair,
Young partridges creep, nestling under his hair,
Brown honey-bees drop something sweet on his lips,
Rash grasshoppers hop on his round finger-tips,
Birds hover above him with musical call ;
All things seem to love him, and he loves them all.

Is nothing afraid of the boy lying there ?
Would all nature aid if he wanted its care ?
Things timid and wild with soft eagerness come.
Ah, poor little child !—he is deaf—he is dumb.
But what can have brought them ? but how can they
        know ?
What instinct has taught them to cherish him so ?

Since first he could walk they have served him like
        this.
His lips could not talk, but they found they could kiss.
They made him a court, and they crowned him a king ;
Ah, who could have thought of so lovely a thing ?
They found him so pretty, they gave him their hearts,
And some divine pity has taught them their parts !

                                        " A."

A DREAM'S AWAKENING.

SHUT in a close and dreary sleep,
    Lonely and frightened and oppressed,
I felt a dreadful serpent creep,
    Writhing and crushing, o'er my breast.

I woke, and knew my child's sweet arm,
　As soft and pure as flakes of snow,
Beneath my dream's dark, hateful charm,
　Had been the thing that tortured so.

And, in the morning's dew and light,
　I seemed to hear an angel say,
"The Pain that stings in Time's low night
　May prove God's Love in higher day."

S. M. B. Piatt.

QUESTIONS OF THE HOUR.

"Do angels wear white dresses, say?
　Always, or only in the summer?　Do
Their birthdays have to come like mine, in May?
　Do they have scarlet sashes then, or blue?

"When little Jessie died last night,
　How could she walk to Heaven—it is so far?
How did she find the way without a light?
　There wasn't even any moon or star.

"Will she have red or golden wings?
　Then will she have to be a bird, and fly?
Do they take men like presidents and kings
　In hearses with black plumes clear to the sky?

"How old is God?　Has he grey hair?
　Can he see yet?　Where did He have to stay
Before—you know—He had made—Anywhere?
　Who does He pray to—when He has to pray?

" How many drops are in the sea?
   How many stars?—well, then, you ought to know
How many flowers are on an apple-tree?
   How does the wind look when it doesn't blow?

" Where does the rainbow end?   And why
   Did—Captain Kidd—bury the gold there?   When
Will this world burn?   And will the firemen try
   To put the fire out with the engines then?

" If you should ever die, may we
   Have pumpkins growing in the garden, so
My fairy godmother can come for me,
   When there's a prince's ball, and let me go?

" Read Cinderella just once more—
   What makes—men's other wives—so mean?"   I
      know
That I was tired, it may be cross, before
   I shut the printed book for her to go."

Hours later, from a child's white bed
   I heard the timid, last queer question start :
" Mamma, are you—my stepmother?" it said.
   The innocent reproof crept to my heart.

                                    S. M. B. Piatt.

MY ARTIST.

So slight, and just a little vain,
   Of eyes and amber-tinted hair
Such as you will not see again—
   To watch him at the window there,

Why, you would not expect, I say,
The rising rival of Doré.

No sullen lord of foreign verse
    Such as great Dante, yet he knows ;
No Wandering Jew's long legend-curse
    On his light hand its darkness throws ,
Nor has the Bible suffered much
So far, from his irreverent touch.

Yet, can his restless pencil lack
    A master Fancy, weird and strong
In black-and-white—but chiefly black !--
    When at its call such horrors throng?
What Fantasies of Fairyland
More shadowy were ever planned ?

But giants and enchantments make
    Not all the glory of his Art :
His vast and varied power can take
    In real things a real part.
His latest pictures here I see :
Will you not look at some with me ?

First, "Alexander."   From his wars,
    With arms of awful length he seems
To reach some very-pointed stars,
    As if "more worlds" were in his dreams !
But, hush—the Artist tells us why :
"You read—'His hands could touch the sky.' "

Here—mark how marvellous, how new !—
    Above a drowning ship, at night,
Close to the moon the sun shines, too,
    While lightnings show in streaks of white—

Still, should my eyes grow dim, ah, then
Their tears will wet those sinking men !

There in wild weather, quite forlorn,
    And queer of cloak, and grim of hat,
With locks that might be better shorn,
    High as a steeple—who is that ?
"It is the man who—I forget—
Stood on a tower in the wet."

His faults ?   He yet is young, you know—
    Four with his last year's butterflies.
But think what wonders books may show
    When the new Tennysons arise !
For fame that he might illustrate
Let poets be content to wait !

S. M. B. Piatt.

LAST WORDS

Over a little bed at night.

GOOD NIGHT, pretty sleepers of mine—
    I never shall see you again :
Ah, never in shadow or shine ;
    Ah never in dew or in rain.

In your small dreaming-dresses of white,
    With the wild-bloom you gathered to-day
In your quiet shut hands, from the light
    And the dark you will wander away.

Though no graves in the bee-haunted grass,
  And no love in the beautiful sky,
Shall take you as yet, you will pass,
  With this kiss, through these tear-drops.
    Good-bye !

With less gold and more gloom in their hair,
  When the buds near have faded to flowers,
Three faces may wake here as fair—
  But older than yours are, by hours !

Good night, then, lost darlings of mine—
  I never shall see you again :
Ah, never in shadow or shine,
  Ah, never in dew or in rain.

S. M. B. Piatt.

TO MARIAN, ASLEEP.

THE full moon glimmers still and white,
  Where yon shadowy clouds unfold ;
The stars, like children of the night,
  Lie with their little heads of gold
On her dark lap : nor less divine,
And brighter, seems your own on mine.

My darling, with your snowy sleep
  Folded around your dimpled form,
Your little breathings calm and deep,
  Your mother's arms and heart are warm ;
You wear as lilies in your breast
The dreams that blossom from your rest.

Ah, must your clear eyes see ere long
   The mist and wreck on sea and land,
And that old haunter of all song,
   The mirage hiding in the sand?
And with the dead leaves in the frost
Tell you of song and summer lost?

And shall you hear the ghastly tales
   From the slow, solemn lips of Time—
Of Wrong that wins, of Right that fails,
   Of trampled Want and gorgeous Crime,
Of Splendour's glare in lighted rooms,
And Famine's moan in outer glooms?

Of armies in their red eclipse
   That mingle on the smoking plain ;
Of storms that dash our mighty ships
   With silks and spices through the main ;
Of what it costs to climb or fall—
Of Death's great Shadow, ending all?

But, baby Marian, do I string
   The dusk with darker rhymes for you,
Forgetting that you came in Spring,
   The child of sun and bloom and dew,
And that I kissed, still fresh to-day,
The rosiest bud of last year's May?

Forgive me, pretty one : I know,
   Whatever sufferings onward lie,
Christ wore his crown of thorns below
   To gain his crown of light on high ;
And when the lamp's frail flame is gone,
Look up ! the stars will still shine on.

               S. M. B. Piatt.

THE GIRL'S MORNING PRAYER.

SHE rose from her untroubled sleep,
  And put away her soft-brown hair,
And in a tone as low and deep
  As love's first whisper, breathed a prayer.
Her snow-white hands together pressed,
  Her blue eyes cast upon the ground,
The hands held up before her breast,
  She inward prayed without a sound.
And from her long and flowing dress
  Escaped the bare and slender feet,
Whose shape upon the earth did press
  Like the new snow-flakes, white and sweet,
And then, from slumber pure and warm,
  Like a young spirit fresh from heaven,
She bowed her slight and graceful form,
  And humbly prayed to be forgiven:
She prayed for father and for mother,
And begged for all to love each other.

O God ! if souls unsoiled as these
  Need daily mercy from thy throne ;
If she upon her bended knees,
  Our loveliest and our purest one,
She with a face so clear and bright,
We deem her some stray child of light ;

If she with those soft eyes in tears,
Day after day in her first years,
  Must kneel and pray for grace from Thee,
  What far, far deeper need have we !
How hardly, if she win not heaven,
Will *our* transgressions be forgiven !

The Author of " A Child's Life."

THE THINGS IN THE CHILDREN'S DRAWER.

THERE are whips and tops and pieces of strings,
  There are shoes which no little feet wear,
There are bits of ribbon and broken rings,
  And tresses of golden hair ;
There are little dresses folded away
Out of the light of the sunny day.

There are dainty jackets that never are worn,
  There are toys and models of ships,
There are books and pictures all faded and torn,
  And marked by the finger tips
Of dimpled hands that have fallen to dust ;
Yet I strive to think that the Lord is just.

But a feeling of bitterness fills my soul
  Sometimes, when I try to pray,
That the reaper has spared so many flowers
  And taken mine away ; .
And I almost doubt if the Lord can know
That a mother's heart can love them so.

Then I think of the many weary ones
  Who are waiting and watching to-night
For the slow return of faltering feet
  That have strayed from paths of right ;
Who have darkened their lives by shame and sin,
Whom the snares of the tempter have gathered in.

They wander far in distant climes,
  They perish by fire and flood,
And their hands are black with the direst crimes
  That kindled the wrath of God.
Yet a mother's song has soothed them to rest:
She hath lulled them to slumber upon her breast.

And then I think of my children two—
  My babes that never grew old ;
To know they are waiting and watching for you,
  In the city with streets of gold !
Safe, safe from the cares of the weary years,
  From sorrow and sin and war ;
And I thank my God with falling tears
  For the things in the bottom drawer.
                    The Author of " A Child's Life."

TO MY DAUGHTER.

THOU hast the colours of the spring,
The gold of kingcups triumphing,
  The blue of wood-bells wild ;
But winter-thoughts thy spirit fill,
And thou art wandering from us still,
  Too young to be our child.

Yet have thy fleeting smiles confessed,
Thou dear and much-desirèd guest,
  That home is near at last ;
Long lost in high mysterious lands,
Close by our door thy spirit stands,
  Its journey well-nigh past.

Oh sweet bewildered soul, I watch
The fountains of thine eyes, to catch
  New fancies bubbling there,
To feel our common light, and lose
The flush of strange ethereal hues
  Too dim for us to share ;

Fade, cold immortal lights, and make
This creature human for my sake,
   Since I am nought but clay;
An angel is too fine a thing
To sit beside my chair and sing,
   And cheer my passing day.

I smile, who could not smile, unless
The air of rapt unconsciousness
   Passed, with the fading hours;
I joy in every childish sign
That proves the stranger less divine
   And much more meekly ours.

I smile, as one by night who sees,
Through mist of newly-budded trees,
   The clear Orion set,
And knows that soon the dawn will fly
In fire across the riven sky,
   And gild the woodlands wet.

Edmund Gosse.

SPILLENDE GENIER.

(A BAS-RELIEF OF THORWALDSEN'S.)

SEE, there is silence now! The harmony,
   Drawn out into a long delicious close,
   Falls gently, as the petals of a rose
Drop silently at night into the sea;
The moon that climbs behind the poplar-tree,

And therein like a ghostly blossom glows,
Has waited patiently until she knows
That rest is brooding round the god-like three.
Ah ! little trinity of light and song,
What earth, what heaven can claim you ?   O delay !
Still let your curvèd fingers wind along
The trembling strings that quiver while you play !
Let not my earthly presence do you wrong !
I move not, speak not, lest you fade away !

But ah ! one sweet child, turning, waves his wings,
And lifts his magian harp into the air ;
Can those be tears that glimmer in his hair,
Fast fallen from his eyes' pure water springs?
His fingers falter soft athwart the strings ;
The melody is more than heart can bear,
It ravels all the threads of pain and care,
And, to dissolve the rhythmic bond, he sings.
It seems as though a bird, too sad to mourn
When all its happier mates are fled and flown,
Should sing old spring-songs to a winter grove :
Eldest and saddest of the three, forlorn
Of dreams and fancies, he has slowly grown
The soul and image of the antique Love.

But, see, his brother, laughing, folds his plumes,
And strikes a chord upon his viol-wires ;
No anthem this of faded hearts' desires,
Or life's wan ghost, that walks among the tombs ;
And he who holds the golden pipe resumes
His mellow music, and a song aspires
From both in unison, as when the choirs
Of Venus' maidens sing above their looms.
For these are Hope, that pipes our lives away,
And Pleasure, with his plectrum, sweet desire .

37

Love stands apart, and sadder far than they,
  For he has tasted deeper life and higher,
  And seen the eyes of Pleasure lose their fire,
And Hope, delayed past hoping for, decay.

                    Edmund Gosse.

TO TERESA.

DEAR child of mine, the wealth of whose warm hair
Hangs like ripe clusters of the apricot,
  Thy blue eyes, gazing, comprehend me not,
But love me, and for love alone I care ;
Thou listenest with a shy and serious air,
  Like some Sabrina from her weedy grot
  Outpeeping coyly when the noon is hot
To watch some shepherd piping unaware.
'Twas not for thee I sang, dear child ;—and yet
  Would that my song could reach such ears as thine,
Pierce to young hearts unsullied by the fret
  Of years in their white innocence divine ;
Crowned with a wreath of buds still dewy-wet,
  O what a fragrant coronal were mine !

                    Edmund Gosse.

AT CHAMBERS.

To the chamber, where now uncaring
  I sit apart from the strife,
While the fool and the knave are sharing.
  The pleasures and profits of life,

There came a faint knock at the door,
    Not long since on a terrible day ;
One faint little knock, and no more ;
    And I brushed the loose papers away.

And as no one made answer, I rose,
    With quick step and impatience of look,
And a glance of the eye which froze,
    And a ready voice of rebuke.

But when the door opened, behold !
    A mother, low-voiced and mild,
Whose thin shawl and weak arms enfold
    A pale little two-year-old child.

What brought her there ?   Would I relieve her ?
    Was all the poor mother could say :
For her child, scarce recovered from fever,
    Left the hospital only that day.

Pale indeed was the child, yet so cheerful,
    That, seeing me wonder, she said,
Of doubt and repulse grown fearful,
    " Please look at his dear little head ; "

And snatched off the little bonnet,
    And so in a moment laid bare
A shorn little head, and upon it
    No trace of the newly-come hair.

When, seeing the stranger's eye
    Grow soft, with an innocent guile
The child looked up, shrinking and shy,
    With the ghost of a baby smile.

Poor child ! I thought, so soon come
   To the knowledge of lives oppressed,
To whom poverty comes with home,
   And sickness brings food and rest :

Who art launched forth, a frail little boat,
   In the midst of life's turbulent sea,
To be sunk, it may be, or to float
   On great waves that care nothing for thee.

What awaits thee?   An early peace
   In the depth of a little grave,
Or, despite all thy ills, to increase,
   Through some dark chance, mighty to save ;

Till in stalwart manhood you meet
   The strong man, who regards you to-day,
Crawling slowly along the street,
   In old age withered and grey ?

Who knows ?   But the thoughts I have told
   In one instant flashed through my brain,
As the poor mother, careful of cold,
   Clasped her infant to her again.

And I, if I searched for my purse,
   Was I selfish, say you, and wrong ?
Surely silver is wasted worse
   Than in earning a right to a song.

                        Lewis Morris.

YOUNG NIGHT THOUGHT.

ALL night long and every night,
When my mamma puts out the light,
I see the people marching by,
As plain as day, before my eye.

Armies and emperors and kings,
And carrying different kinds of things,
And marching in so grand a way,
You never saw the like by day.

So fine a show was never seen
At the great circus on the green ;
For every kind of beast and man
Is marching in that caravan.

At first they move a little slow,
But still the faster on they go,
And still beside them close I keep
Until we reach the town of sleep.

Robert Louis Stevenson.

THE LAND OF COUNTERPANE.

WHEN I was sick and lay a-bed,
I had two pillows at my head,
And all my toys behind me lay
To keep me happy all the day.

And sometimes for an hour or so
I watched my leaden soldiers go,
With different uniforms and drills,
Among the bed-clothes, through the hills ;

And sometimes sent my ships in fleets,
All up and down among the sheets;
Or brought my trees and houses out,
And planted cities all about.

I was the giant great and still
That sits upon the pillow-hill,
And sees before him, dale and plain,
The pleasant land of counterpane.

Robert Louis Stevenson.

ESCAPE AT BEDTIME.

THE lights from the parlour and kitchen shone out
  Through the blinds and the windows and bars;
And high overhead and all moving about,
  There were thousands of millions of stars.
There ne'er were such thousands of leaves on a tree,
  Nor of people in church or the Park,
As the crowds of the stars that looked down upon me,
  And that glittered and winked in the dark.

The Dog, and the Plough, and the Hunter, and all,
  And the star of the sailor, and Mars,
These shone in the sky, and the pail by the wall
  Would be half full of water and stars.
They saw me at last, and they chased me with cries,
  And they soon had me packed into bed;
But the glory kept shining and bright in my eyes,
  And the stars going round in my head.

Robert Louis Stevenson.

MY BED IS A BOAT.

My bed is like a little boat ;
　Nurse helps me in when I embark ;
She girds me in my sailor's coat
　And starts me in the dark.

At night, I go on board and say
　Good night to all my friends on shore :
I shut my eyes and sail away,
　And see and hear no more.

And sometimes things to bed I take,
　As prudent sailors have to do :
Perhaps a slice of wedding-cake,
　Perhaps a toy or two.

All night across the dark we steer :
　But when the day returns at last,
Safe in my room, beside the pier,
　I find my vessel fast.

Robert Louis Stevenson.

THE UNKNOWN TONGUE.

That baby, I knew her in days of old.
You doubt that I lived in a land made fair
With many soft moons, and was mated there ?
Now mark you ! I saw but to-day in the street
A sweet girl-baby, whose delicate feet
As yet upon earth took but uncertain hold ;

Yet she carried a doll as she toddled alone,
And she talked to that doll in a tongue her own.
The sweet little stranger ! why, her face still bore
The look of the people from the far star-shore.

Ah ! you doubt me still? then listen : While you
Have looked to the earth for gold, why I——
I have looked to the steeps of the starry sky.
And which, indeed, had the fairer view
Of the infinite things, the dreamer or you ? . . .
How blind be men when they will not see !
If men must look in the dust, or look
At best, with the eyes bound down to a book,
Why, who shall deny that it comes to me
To sail white ships through the ether sea ?

Yes, I am a dreamer.   Yet, while you dream,
Then I am awake.   When a child, back through
The gates of the past I peered, and I knew
The land I had lived in.   I saw the broad stream ;
Saw rainbows that compassed a world in their reach ;
I saw my belovèd go down on the beach ;
Saw her lean to this earth, saw her looking for me
As shipmen look from their ships at sea. . . .
The sweet girl-baby !   Why, that unknown tongue
Is the tongue she has talked since the stars were
        young !

Joaquin Miller.

CHRISTMAS EVE.

ONE eve, when the cold snow lay white
    Along the silent street,
A little child, all clothed in light
    And with a smile most sweet,

Did enter my dim lonely room
  As chimed the midnight bell :—
" I am thy Life, thy Death, thy Doom,
  For thee I entered Hell ! "

" O little child," I said, " art thou
  Some messenger divine ? "
He pointed to his tender brow
  Round which soft light did shine,

And there I saw a shadowy crown,
  Of plaited thorns 'twas wrought,
And from each thorn there tickled down
  A liquid crimson spot.

And while I looked he faded slow
  And vanish'd from my sight :
Only the gusty wind did blow
  The wild snow through the night.

And when in after-dreams I lay
  I heard the white hosts cry,
" Hosanna ! on this day
  The Christ comes from on high ! "

William Sharp.

THE STREET CHILDREN'S DANCE.

Now the earth in fields and hills
Stirs with pulses of the Spring,
Nest-embowering hedges ring
With interminable trills ;
Sunlight runs a race with rain,
All the world grows young again.

Young as at the hour of birth :
From the grass the daisies rise
With the dew upon their eyes,
Sun-awakened eyes of earth ;
Fields are set with cups of gold ;
Can this budding world grow old ?

Can the world grow old and sere,
Now when ruddy-tasselled trees
Stoop to every passing breeze,
Rustling in their silken gear ;
Now when blossoms pink and white
Have their own celestial light ?

Brooding light falls soft and warm,
Where in many a wind-rocked nest,
Curled up 'neath the she-bird's breast,
Clustering eggs are hid from harm ;
While the mellow-throated thrush
Warbles in the purpling bush.

Misty purple bathes the Spring :
Swallows flashing here and there
Float and dive on waves of air,
And make love upon the wing ;
Crocus-buds in sheaths of gold
Burst like sunbeams from the mould.

Chestnut leaflets burst their buds, ·
Perching tiptoe on each spray,
Springing toward the radiant day,
As the bland pacific floods
Of the generative sun
All the teeming earth o'errun.

Can this earth run o'er with beauty,
Laugh through leaf and flower and grain,
While in close-pent court and lane,
In the air so thick and sooty,
Little ones pace to and fro,
Weighted with their parent's woe?

Woe-predestined little ones !
Putting forth their buds of life
In an atmosphere of strife,
And crime-breeding ignorance ;
Where the bitter surge of care
Freezes to a dull despair.

Dull despair and misery
Lies about them from their birth ;
Ugly curses, uglier mirth,
Are their earliest lullaby ;
Fathers have they without name,
Mothers crushed by want and shame.

Brutish, overburdened mothers,
With their hungry children cast
Half-nude to the nipping blast ;
Little sisters with their brothers
Dragging in their arms all day
Children nigh as big as they.

Children withered by the street :
Shouting, flouting, roaring after
Passers-by with gibes and laughter,
Diving between horses' feet,
In and out of drays and barrows,
Recklessly, like London sparrows.

Mudlarks of our slums and alleys,
All unconscious of the blooming
World beyond these housetops looming,
Of the happy fields and valleys,
Of the miracle of Spring
With its boundless blossoming.

Blossoms of humanity !
Poor soiled blossoms in the dust !
Through the thick defiling crust
Of soul-stifling poverty,
In your features may be traced
Children's beauty half effaced—

Childhood, stunted in the shadow
Of the light-debarring walls :
Not for you the cuckoo calls
O'er the silver-threaded meadow ;
Not for you the lark on high
Pours his music from the sky.

Ah ! you have your music too !
And come flocking round that player
Grinding at his organ there,
Summer-eyed and swart of hue,
Rattling off his well-worn tune
On this April afternoon.

Lovely April lights of pleasure,
Flit o'er want-beclouded features
Of those little outcast creatures,
As they swing with rhythmic measure,
In the courage of their rags,
Lightly o'er the slippery flags.

Little footfalls, lightly glancing
In a luxury of motion,
Supple as the waves of ocean,
In your elemental dancing,
How you fly, and wheel, and spin,
For your hearts too dance within !

Dance along with mirth and laughter,
Buoyant, fearless and elate,
Dancing in the teeth of fate,
Ignorant of your hereafter,
That with all its tragic glooms
Blinding on your future looms.

Past and future, hence away !
Joy, diffused throughout all the earth,
Centre in this moment's mirth
Of ecstatic holiday :
Once in all their live's dark story
Touch them, Fate ! with April glory !

Mathilde Blind.

THE SCHOOL CHILDREN.

THESE at least are clean and fresh,
   All I wished to see !
Hair a flaxen flossy mesh,
   Waving loose and free
Round their ruddy English flesh.

Now at last they're out of school,
   Happy, happy time.
Now a truce to book and rule,
   Task in prose or rhyme,
Thought of prize or dunce's stool.

How they laugh and run about !
   What if now and then
Somewhat overloud a shout
   Reach you busier men ;
Could the children play without ?

What, you call them rude and rough,
   Overprone to strife ?
Still I find them good enough
   For such eager life ;
What should they be thinking of ?

Though they know a mint of things,
   So their mothers say,
Read and write, and rattle strings
   And strings of dates away,
Bible judges, English kings,

I, for one, should never dare
   Such a gage to fate,
As to stand with any there
   Pouring name and date,
Faster, faster . . . O despair !

That one passed in Euclid, look !
   This can draw and sing !
And the girls, I think, can cook
   Any mortal thing :
So they quote their cookery-book.

Ay—you cry—too much they know
   For their lowlier rank ;
Teach them but to plant and hoe,
   But to beg and thank,
For the clown needs keeping low.

Nay, but listen, neighbour, pray—
  Once a Flemish seer,
David Joris, so they say,
  Saw in trance appear
Kings and knights in great array ;

Through his twilit painting-room
  Stalk the sombre host,
Priests and prelates grandly loom—
  Every one a ghost,
Silent as the silent gloom.

Very sad and overworn,
  Pale and very old,
Look the solemn brows that mourn
  Under crowns of gold,
Grown too heavy to be borne.

Kings and priests, and all so grey,
  All so faint and wan,
Drifting past in still array,
  Ever drifting on,
'Till at length he saw them stay.

Saw a second vision rise
  Through the twilit air,
Heard what laughter and lisping cries,
  Saw what tumbled hair,
Rosy limbs and rounded eyes !

Playing children—much the same
  As we see them here,
Laughing in a merry game—
  Rose before him clear ;
But they clove the dusk like flame.

Heeding not the ghostly throng,
  David heard them sing ;
At the echo of their song
  Saw each ghostly king
Lift his eyes, look hard and long.

Till at length, as when a breeze
  Bends the rushes well,
Captains, kings, great sovereignties,
  Bent, and bowed, and fell
Kneeling upon all their knees.

Laying at the children's feet
  Each his kingly crown,
Each, the conquering power to greet,
  Laying humbly down
Sword and sceptre, as is meet.

Then, unkinged and dispossessed,
  Rose the weary host,
Glad at last to cease and rest,
  For to every ghost
Comes the time when peace is best.

Since our crown must fall to them,
  When beyond our reach
Falls our dearest diadem,
  Neighbour, let us teach
Every child to prize the gem

For, be sure, the new things grow
  As the old things fade.
As we train the children, so
  Is the future made
That shall reign when we are low.

All the work we would have wrought
   Must by them be done ;
We shall pass, but not our thought ;
   While in every one
Lives the lesson that we taught.

A. Mary F. Robinson.

Printed by WALTER SCOTT, Felling, Newcastle-on-Tyne.

The Camelot Classics.

PROSPECTUS.

THE main idea in instituting this Edition is to provide the general reader with a comprehensive Prose Library after his own heart,—an Edition, that is to say, cheap, without the reproach which cheapness usually implies, comprising volumes of shapely form, well printed, well bound, and thoroughly representative of the leading prose writers of all time. Placed thus upon a popular basis, making the principle of literary selection a broadly human rather than an academic one, the Edition will, the Publisher hopes, contest not ineffectually the critical suffrages of the democratic shilling.

As in the CANTERBURY POETS issued from the same press, to which this aims at being a companion series, the *Editing* of the volumes will be a special feature. This will be entrusted to writers who will each, in freshly treated, suggestive Introductions, give just that account of the book and its author which will enable the significance of both in life and literature, and their relation to modern thought, to be readily grasped. And where, for the successful rescue of old-time books for modern reading, revision and selection are necessary, the editing will be done with careful zeal and with reverence always for the true spirit of the book. In the first volume a General Introduction by the Editor will appear, explaining more fully the bearing of the series, which, in course of time, it is hoped, will form

A COMPLETE PROSE LIBRARY FOR THE PEOPLE.

Just Published, Paper Covers, 1s.; Cloth, 1s. 6d.

THE

HEATHER ON FIRE:

A TALE OF THE HIGHLAND CLEARANCES.

POEM

By MATHILDE BLIND.

LONDON:

WALTER SCOTT, 24 WARWICK LANE,

PATERNOSTER ROW.

www.ingramcontent.com/pod-product-compliance
Lightning Source LLC
Chambersburg PA
CBHW060538030726
47498CB00004B/1235